'I am going to make the Captain fall in love with me. And when he does I shall reject him utterly and there will be nothing he can do about it.'

When Napoleon's army occupies Vienna in the winter of 1805, Léon de Vaudry, Captain of the Dragoons, finds himself a billet at the home of a Viennese Baroness. Her daughter Stephanie is horrified at the very idea of a Frenchman in their midst and determines to shatter the dashing Captain's infuriating self-esteem. But she soon finds her strategy has not at all the desired effect . . .

The Emperor's Dragoon

Ann Hulme

MILLS & BOON LIMITED
London · Sydney · Toronto

First published 1983

© Ann Hulme 1983

Australian copyright 1983

ISBN 0 263 10343 9

095475

Set in 10/10½ pt Linotron Times
08/0883

*Photoset by Rowland Phototypesetting Ltd
Bury St Edmunds, Suffolk
Made and printed in Great Britain by
Richard Clay (The Chaucer Press) Ltd,
Bungay, Suffolk*

CHAPTER
ONE

'I SUPPOSE,' Stefanie remarked, 'that it is possible to dance away dishonour?'

The yellow glow cast by innumerable candles glittered down through the crystal droplets of the great chandeliers like a shower of golden rain above the splendid rococo ballroom with its pink and white stucco and carved and gilded panels. The Baroness was giving a party, the last before leaving Vienna with her two daughters to spend the rest of the winter on the family's Moravian estate.

All evening the orchestra had been busy playing popular dances one after the other, quadrille, polka, schottische, and the waltz, of course the waltz, scandalising, shocking, but permeating the whole of Viennese society with its gay momentum. Dancers and orchestra were equally exhausted. But now the clock had struck eleven, and they could all take a rest, knowing that, when they recommenced, they would play and dance until four in the morning. The musicians laid aside their instruments and took themselves off gratefully to the room where refreshment had been set out for them. New arrivals, a Hungarian gipsy orchestra, engaged to play for the guests during supper, took the vacant places, trundling in a *cimbálom* to add its melancholy tinkling to the tune they struck up on their fiddles.

The dancers made their way, chattering and laughing, towards supper tables groaning beneath a lavish spread. The room was filled with handsome men and beautiful women, an ever changing rainbow of magnificent uniforms and silken gowns. Trays of ices had been offered to the dancers between their exertions, for tiled stoves had heated the air until the atmosphere had become oppressive, and the Baroness signalled now to a footman to open one of the great windows looking out towards the still standing ramparts of the city.

Stefanie, the elder of the Baroness' two lovely daughters, flicked open a fan of delicate carved ivory in a silver clasp, and moved it gently to and fro as she made her remark to her mother. The current of air created was warm and unpleasant, not in the least cooling. Stefanie sighed and snapped the little fan shut impatiently.

'You will break it,' admonished her mother in an absent, automatic way. Her attention was elsewhere. She had not heard her daughter's comment.

'I said,' Stefanie raised her voice slightly, 'that Vienna dances. Who would think that we are surrounded by disaster and defeat, with Napoleon himself sitting upon our very borders!'

'Indeed,' murmured the Baroness, 'one must believe the Corsican upstart in league with the devil! Our poor, gallant soldiers . . .'

Stefanie shrugged and spread open the little fan. From behind its cover, she observed the debonair young officers who represented the defeated Austrian army there that evening. It was true that those handsome young faces had lost some of the buoyant enthusiasm of a few months earlier. The smiles they wore were perhaps a little forced now. Superficially they were the same charming, elegant and dashing young escorts, leading their pretty partners through the dances, only the hint of a new earnestness in their eyes betrayed the fact that they were wretchedly conscious of the disgrace which besmirched their names and that of Austria herself.

Many of those same young men glanced longingly from time to time at the slim, beautiful girl in the ballgown of white and silver, pearls braided in her golden curls, who stood beside her mother watching them so quizzically. They looked at her, and then they looked at each other and smiled ruefully. Stefanie saw it and understood. She knew what name they had given her amongst themselves. They called her 'the Snow-maiden'—whose heart was icy and unrelenting, after whom they could all sigh, but whom none could hope to conquer.

'They say I cannot fall in love, as if it were somehow all my fault!' thought Stefanie rebelliously. 'But I cannot fall in love just because it is expected of me. I am not afraid of being in love, but I am twenty-two and past girlish infatuations. When I fall in love, it will be for ever, that much I know! But for that I must first meet a man for whom I could feel I was *meant*. I wonder if that is what Magda feels for Andreas . . .'

She looked towards her younger sister, pretty, dark-haired Maria-Magdalena, whom everyone called Magda, and who was gazing adoringly at a slim, attractive youth in the elaborate uniform of the Austrian Hussars.

It was this sight which was the object of the Baroness' attention. She gave an exclamation of annoyance, following it by tapping sharply with her own fan on Stefanie's arm.

'Stefanie, child, do go and speak to Magda! Stop her mooning like that in front of everyone. I swear, she has not left young von Letzberg's side all evening. She hangs on his arm and they spend their time staring at each other like a pair of lovestruck rustics. Kindly go and remind your sister that she has duties towards *other* guests here. Try and prise young von Letzberg away. It becomes embarrassing!'

Stefanie burst into laughter. 'Mama, how can you be so cruel? Poor Magda and Andreas are in love!'

'Love? What do they know of love?' cried the Baroness angrily. 'They are children. Magda has not yet seen her eighteenth birthday and von Letzberg is scarcely twenty. Love, indeed!' The Baroness snorted. 'The next thing we know, they will be wanting to be engaged.'

'Is that so bad, Mama? You can't object to Andreas, surely? His uncle, Hofrat von Letzberg, is one of your oldest friends.' Stefanie accompanied this with a sly look at her mother.

The Baroness, a handsome widow who, at four and forty, had kept her figure and was proud of her unlined forehead and hair untouched by grey, was unmollified. 'Of course I don't object to Andreas himself. He is a dear boy. But for goodness' sake, Stefanie, you know perfectly well that the Austrian army does not allow its officers to marry unless they can show themselves able to support a wife in suitable style, and quite rightly. One cannot have people of position and quality living on the smell of a herring in a pair of rented rooms.'

'The von Letzbergs are not poor. Besides, perhaps his uncle will do something for Andreas.'

'He might . . . in his will! That, please God, will not be read for some years yet. As for the von Letzbergs, there are just too many of them. Andreas has two brothers who will want their share, and three marriageable sisters who will want a dowry apiece. When a family fortune is carved up like that into as many small pieces as the beef for a goulash, what's to be left for anyone?' demanded the Baroness despairingly.

Seeing her mother was not to be placated, Stefanie left her side and went smiling towards her sister and the young man in question.

'Now, my children,' she said with mock severity, taking each of them by the hand. 'What am I to do? Here I am, dispatched by Mama with the strictest instructions, Lieutenant von Letzberg, to detach you from my sister. And you, Magda my pet, are to go and talk to everyone and anyone—only not to poor Andreas here!'

'Is Mama being difficult?' asked Magda apprehensively.

'No. She is simply asking you to look after *all* our guests,' Stefanie told her sternly.

'Don't scold Magda, it is my fault,' the young man said contritely. 'I saw your mother looking at us just now. I should have moved away and started saying some gallant nonsense to someone else.' He pushed back his curly mop of light brown hair and gave a wry grimace.

'I shouldn't have liked that,' objected Magda with engaging candour, turning her charming little face up to his.

'I shouldn't have meant it,' he assured her earnestly. 'Not to anyone but you!'

'Indeed,' thought Stefanie in some exasperation, 'they *are* children . . . and so in love, it shines out of their eyes like stars! What's to be done?' Unbidden, the sad little wish crossed her mind, 'and if it could only be said of me, too. If I had someone to love like this . . .'

'It is because Andreas has no money,' Magda said now dejectedly.

'Ah, but I shall!' he said with the optimism of youth. 'When my uncle dies. I know that sounds callous, and I certainly don't want the poor old fellow dead, but I *am* his heir. He's told me so a hundred times. He has left me his entire Styrian estates.'

'But not yet!' Stefanie reminded him, wagging a reproving forefinger.

'Well, in the meantime, I shall cover myself with glory, see if I don't,' he returned undaunted. 'That business at Ulm, it was all a mistake.' With a generous wave of his hand he dismissed the recent humiliating surrender of the Austrian forces under General Mack at Ulm in Bavaria. 'General Mack was too old and took fright when he saw the Grand Army! But it won't happen again. Next time we'll trounce Napoleon and his

Grand Army, and send them all scampering back to France! And I shall get the order of Maria Theresa and be a national hero!' He grinned with boyish enthusiasm.

'You may have your opportunity to be that very soon, young man!' observed the Baroness, joining them. 'So I advise you to save your ardour for the glories of battle. My daughter will survive very well without your attentions.'

'I don't like to think of Andreas in the middle of a battle,' said Magda nervously. 'He could be in such danger.'

'But, don't you see?' he urged anxiously. 'How else am I to get my chance? We must show them Austria is not beaten. And now the Russians . . .'

He was interrupted. Their talk had attracted the attention of others about them.

'Why, you don't have anything to fear, *gnädiges Fräulein*!' cried an Uhlan sporting ferocious, warlike moustachios. 'Napoleon has made the greatest mistake of his career in violating our borders. Now he has to fight not only our Austrian army, but our Russian allies, too! Don't forget, Kutuzov's Russians stand between Napoleon and Vienna. Our combined armies will rout the French utterly! Every man will kill his Frenchman, or two or three!'

'We may feel quite safe, then, here in Vienna?' Stefanie asked, listening to this bloodthirsty prophecy.

'Dear Fräulein Stefanie!' cried the owner of another splendid uniform, for now they were the centre of an excited crowd. 'Will we allow the upstart Bonaparte to gobble up Vienna? He'll choke on that morsel. The Russians cannot allow Vienna to fall. They will stand by us. They already bar the route to Vienna. Any day, dear ladies, and you will receive the news of a tremendous Allied victory, Napoleon in disarray and his army annihilated! Long live the Emperor Franz!'

The cry was taken up and the chandeliers rang with 'Long live the Emperor Franz!' rising from a hundred throats.

Stefanie felt a tide of exhilaration surge through her. It must be true—they were on the eve of a great victory! She heard her own voice adding to the enthusiastic cries of the rest.

'Then, my dear friends,' said the Baroness graciously, as the cheering died away, 'we must indeed be grateful that our Russian allies have come to help us. Now . . . let us go into supper. Let there be no more talk of war this evening.'

The crowd dispersed and soon the tinkling of glass and china was added to the chatter and laughter. The gipsy orchestra, which had stopped playing during the cheering, took up their instruments again. Stefanie, who stood nearby, turned towards them. The leader of the orchestra, the *primás*, struck a low, throbbing note on his violin, which was taken up by the others. The expression on his brown, wrinkled face was unfathomable. For him there was only the music. But the *cimbálom* player sat motionless behind his instrument, watching the crowd of guests. Stefanie was struck by the expression in his dark eyes. They twinkled with merriment. He was laughing, yes, laughing . . . not at some joke, but quite simply at *them*, at all the glittering assembly, laughing at their patriotic pride and the proud boasts of those splendid young men, all athirst for glory and a chance to redeem Austria's honour. Nor was it a kindly and indulgent merriment. No, it was a malicious and knowing laughter and it struck a sudden chill in Stefanie's heart.

'Why, he sees us as fools and braggarts!' she exclaimed to herself. From the height of exhilaration, she was suddenly plunged into an agony of apprehension and dread. What *did* he see, that dark-eyed gipsy with the swarthy, pock-marked skin and luxuriant moustaches? Could he see into the future, as his race was reputed able to do? If so, what kind of future? Stefanie shook herself angrily. Why, was she to be frightened by a gipsy musician? It was childish nonsense, reminiscent of the days when, as a little girl, she had watched the bands of gipsies pass through the little villages around her family's estate in Moravia. Colourful, enigmatic, sharp-eyed and light-fingered, they would arrive one day from over the horizon and disappear the next, no one knew where. As for this fellow, he no doubt laughed for some reason easily explained. He had, perhaps, overheard some witticism from one of the guests.

She turned her back on him, but every so often she felt her eyes drawn irresistibly back again. No matter with whom she talked, or however animated the conversation, still the gipsy exercised some strange fascination which made her look his way again and again. Each time she saw—or fancied she saw—that mocking laughter gleaming in the dark eyes.

It seemed warmer than ever in the stuffy, overheated ballroom, and she felt she must escape for a few minutes. Smiling and making excuses, she edged past the laughing, chattering couples and slipped out of a small door at the far end into the hall. On the way, she passed Andreas, trying to signal some message to Magda across the room without the Baroness noticing. It was so obvious that in all that throng, those two had eyes only for each other.

'Be patient,' she whispered to him. 'Later, I'll try to distract my mother . . . and you can talk to Magda again.'

Relief crossed his young face and he smiled his thanks at her.

There was nobody in the hall. Everybody was making his or her way towards the supper tables. But not quite all, for the drawing room door was ajar and she could hear male voices in there, raised in some dispute. She did not mean to listen, but just then the voices grew louder, one dominating.

'Oh, I grant you, the Russians are certainly here!' declared the voice aggressively. 'But I have had personal dealings with the generals of the Holy, Imperial Russian Army! It is impossible to pin them down, or get them to divulge any intention or plan whatsoever. One would think they had come all the way from Mother Russia just to plague our Austrian villagers on whom they are billeted. The truth is, they mistrust us. They doubt our ability to fight. Oh, their officers are polite enough to one's face . . . but behind one's back it is a different story. "German sausage-eater", I overheard one impudent young hound call me! A baby-faced cadet fresh out of some military academy, hardly old enough to grow a moustache. I affected not to hear . . .'

The words reminded Stefanie that she, too, should not overhear. She glanced at her reflection in a nearby pierglass, and went back into the ballroom.

As she entered, the *primás* struck the first notes of a melancholy love melody and a trio of Hungarian Hussars who were nearby, magnificent in their sky-blue breeches and gold embroidered and fur-trimmed jackets, their black moustaches waxed and shining, gathered into a little group. Arms about each other's shoulders, they swayed gently to that soft, sensuous music. Perhaps they were moved by that burning nationalism in every Hungarian heart, which served the Emperor only because he wore the crown of St Stephen. Perhaps it was the wine which the Baroness had ordered should flow plenteously. Perhaps it was the memory of pretty girls left behind in a dozen or so dusty villages strung across the wide Puszta . . . but they sang quietly in accompaniment to the throbbing of the violins, the soft, sibilant Magyar sounds murmuring their way gently through the German and French chatter of the fashionable Viennese like the course of a clear and limpid stream through woodland. ·

Suddenly Stefanie felt very much alone in the midst of all that crowd. There was a great yearning in her heart which made it ache. She wanted to feel someone's arms enfold her, but whose? Certainly no one here, not those sentimental young men in fine uniforms who sang so sincerely for a homeland left behind, not their brother officers from every corner of the Austro-Hungarian empire.

'*Only one little girl is my sweet rose . . .*' thought Stefanie sadly, understanding a little of the words. 'Yet I have no one true love anywhere. I begin to feel I never shall. I belong to no one, and can call no one mine.' '*How the good God must love me, to have given you to me . . .*' went the song. Surely she, too, one day would find someone who could stir the Snowmaiden's heart and answer that yearning.

The *primás* grinned, his white teeth flashing in his nutbrown face. With a sudden change of pace, the gipsy orchestra followed his lead into a quick, bright, lively tune which set the feet tapping of all who heard it, and then, without warning, they broke into a *csárdás*. The musicians fiddled like men possessed and the *cimbálom* player leapt to life, his hands flashing up and down his strange, tinkling instrument until it seemed he must, surely, make a mistake. Yet he did not. Faster and faster whirled the music. The Hussars began to laugh. Stefanie's heart lightened and she felt intoxicated by the whirling notes which spun out into the air from the frenzied playing of the gipsies. Faster and faster . . . the laughter grew louder, the guests were calling out in delight and clapping their hands . . . the gipsies, too, were laughing as they played, and the music rushed on, on . . . The stream had become a torrent, splashing and racing over obstacles headlong, so that there were no worries any more, no cares, no aching hearts, no lost loves, no moments of passion remembered with pain, only a magical dizzy cascade of notes.

In the midst of it all, when it seemed the music must reach it wild climax and drag them all into its swirling vortex, the great double doors leading into the ballroom were flung open and a solitary figure stood framed in the doorway.

The *primás* flung up his bow and the music stopped abruptly in mid bar. A deathly silence fell. Everyone turned to face the immensely dignified form of Hofrat von Letzberg as he stepped unsmiling, clad in black, unrelieved except for the sparkling diamonds of a single decoration on his breast, into the great room. No one spoke. It was as if no one breathed, as if they had all been turned to stone by a spell cast as in a fairy tale.

The Baroness rallied first and hastened to greet her old friend—whom Viennese gossips whispered was her lover, but whispered discreetly, for such information, in Vienna, was carefully recorded in police files. He bowed and took her hand to kiss it ceremoniously, then whispered something to her. The watchers—and whose eyes were not on the two figures in the doorway—saw the Baroness turn pale. She questioned him, incredulity on her face, then, when he replied, swayed slightly, almost as if she would faint. He grasped her arm to steady her and they heard her say quietly but firmly: 'No, no, Ignaz, it is quite all right. Please . . . it is not necessary.'

He released her and she turned to face her guests, stretching out her arms towards them as if she would embrace them all. Stefanie, who had hastened forward as she saw her mother sway, stopped, riveted to the spot by a sense of impending disaster.

'My dear friends. . .' the Baroness said, tears in her voice. 'My dear, dear friends. I have to tell you terrible, unbelievable news. The Russian army is withdrawing into Moravia . . . Although our Emperor Franz pleaded in person with Prince Kutuzov to stand and defend

Vienna, it was in vain. We are not to be defended. The road to Vienna lies open to Napoleon and the Grand Army . . . we have been abandoned. Our gates are to be thrown open . . .'

She stopped, overcome for the moment, and in the silence it seemed to Stefanie she heard faintly, in the background, a ripple of isolated notes tinkling from the *cimbálom*. Yet she could not say whether she really heard it, or if it only echoed in her brain.

'Dear friends . . . we are to be an open city . . .' the Baroness cried out. Her voice broke at last and she turned to lean on her old friend's arm. 'We must prepare to receive the French!'

CHAPTER
TWO

It was a bitterly cold day, that thirteenth of November, 1805. Vienna's narrow streets and high buildings channelled the wind into an icy current which struck with the sharpness of a knife edge and belied the pale winter sunshine. Yet it was not the chill wind which kept so many Viennese barricaded in their homes. It was the entry into their city of the army of Napoleon, after days of rumour and false alarms. Even indoors it was impossible not to sense the presence of that moving mass of soldiers, horses and guns which constituted the most glorious—and notorious—body of men in the civilised world. Many citizens had let their curiosity overcome their fear and stood in sheltered spots, silent and wide-eyed, to watch this magnificent free spectacle. They were here! Those wild egalitarians, those dangerous free-thinkers, those seducers of women! (Of all women, of any station, looks and age notwithstanding, whispered the worthy citizens with not unpleasurable feelings of horror.)

But however others might choose to treat the arrival of the French in the city, the Baroness chose to treat it as a day of mourning. The shutters were fastened, the mirrors veiled, and, as they took their early morning coffee in funereal gloom, Stefanie and Magda were obliged to listen to their mother's bitter observations.

'Kutuzov has abandoned us! I have heard it said that when the Russian peasants are pursued by wolves, they lighten the sleigh by throwing their children to the pack.

I can well believe it—for that is what Kutuzov has done to Vienna. He has thrown us to the French wolf to delay his advance! That such a fate should befall us.'

'Indeed, Mama,' said Stefanie unwisely, 'I am sure he would not have done so, had it not been necessary.'

'You will not speak so lightly when those godless revolutionaries swarm over the entire city! We shall be at their mercy!' The Baroness pushed back her chair and stood up. 'I shall go to hear the prayers for peace at the cathedral.'

'I'll come with you, Mama,' said Magda in a small voice, 'and pray, too.'

'For Andreas, I don't doubt,' thought Stefanie with a sigh.

'Very well,' the Baroness agreed. 'But you, Stefanie, had better stay here, in case Hofrat von Letzberg should send a message. No one knows what is going to happen now, and one of us must be at home at all times, just in case.'

The Baroness swept out with Magda in her wake.

As soon as she was sure her mother and sister had left, Stefanie jumped to her feet and ran to throw open the shutters and let the cold clear autumnal light flood into the room. It was ridiculous, she thought, to sit about in a darkened house, lamenting. That could neither alter nor help the situation. The house fronts across the narrow side street were as tightly shuttered as their own. An elderly man, whom she recognised as the *Hausmeister* of the opposite building, shuffled out and made his slow way down the empty street. He went every morning at this time for a glass of schnapps in the tavern round the corner, and he did not intend to let events interfere with this important part of his day. But the grey-painted shutters remained as defensively barred as ever.

There was a crash and a tinkle from behind her, as the maid who was clearing the coffee cups let one fall onto the polished parquet, shattering it.

'Oh, for goodness' sake, do be careful!' Stefanie snapped at her.

'I'm sorry, *gnädiges Fräulein*, but I'm that nervous, I hardly know what I'm doing,' the girl stammered, kneeling to pick up the pieces. 'Cook says the French are all monsters, and we shall be murdered in our beds.'

'What nonsense. Stay in the house and don't go out. You will be quite safe. And tell Cook I say she is not to be frightening everyone with fairy tales.'

She was sorry to be so severe with the girl, but hysteria amongst the maids was something they could well do without. Although there had been panic all over Vienna ever since the fateful news had come. How the ballroom had emptied of uniforms after Hofrat von Letzberg's dramatic message! The gallant Uhlans and Hussars had galloped away towards Brünn or Olmütz, or wherever they hoped to find their regiments, Andreas amongst them. Poor Magda was in the depths of despair, sobbing herself to sleep every night, convinced her ardent young lover would never return.

The Imperial Court had loaded its valuables into every kind of conveyance and set out at top speed into Moravia, followed by a large number of those wealthy enough to leave the city too. Friends had urged the Baroness and her daughters to leave also, but the Baroness, one of the most resolute of women, had reacted with characteristic hauteur.

'Indeed, we *shall* go into Moravia, for that has always been my intention. Every winter we go to our estate, which lies just beyond Austerlitz. It is only a small country house, but the scene of happy memories, for when I was first married it was there that we made our first home together, my dear late husband and I. But as to the date of our departure, that too has been fixed for some weeks. I shall not alter my plans on account of Napoleon Bonaparte! I shall leave neither earlier nor later than I originally intended. We shall neither run out of Vienna like frightened chickens when the fox approaches the hencoop, nor shall we be prevented by the Corsican upstart and his rabble!'

Stefanie knew her mother well enough to realise the Baroness would stand by every word. Not even the entire Grand Army could have forced her to retreat. Besides, even if they had wished to fly with the rest, it might not have been so easy. Andreas' uncle, Hofrat von Letzberg, had called to give his advice on the matter.

'We cannot know how the French will behave when they reach Vienna . . .' he had observed, seated upon a small sofa, with the Baroness and her daughters seated in a semicircle before him, listening attentively. It was, Stefanie had thought, not unlike a schoolmaster and his class. She had watched him as he opened the lid of an exquisite enamelled snuffbox with a practised flick of a manicured thumbnail. 'However, I must say that all reports reaching me agree that the roads into Moravia are quite crammed with people seeking to fly before Bonaparte. Carriages jostle carts of all descriptions, and people of quality must mingle with peasants. All are burdened with their possessions. The nobility take along their works of art, for the French are such avid "collectors"! The peasant takes along his milch cow. Imagine, amongst all these, the soldiers of our retreating Russian allies! Some of them are wounded, some merely cut off from their units, bereft of officers, drunken . . . The peasant fears our Russian ally more than he fears the French enemy! The roads themselves are quagmires, churned by the hooves, the cartwheels, and the heavy guns of the Russian artillery.' Von Letzberg had paused to take snuff deliberately. 'To say nothing of the—ah —distressing sight by the roadside of the Russian dead, whom no one has time to bury . . .'

So they had remained in Vienna. Stefanie was roused from these reflections now by some considerable noise outside the door. It seemed to be coming up the staircase. She could hear the voice of old Joachim, who had served the family forty years man and boy, raised in anger. There was also another voice, louder and harsher, making, it seemed, some peremptory demands, and all interspersed with sundry female shrieks and squeals. Stefanie had begun to move towards the door to deal with whatever emergency had broken out, when Joachim himself appeared before her, far from his usual composed self. His face was as red and angry as a turkey cock, and he bristled with rage.

'I'm sorry I'm obliged to disturb you, *gnädiges Fräulein*, but in all my years I never met with such impudence! I told the fellow to go away, told him twenty times. But he speaks no German and doesn't care anyway. A real rogue! As insolent as you please, the impudent hound!'

'Why, who?' cried Stefanie, bewildered. 'Who is he and what does he want?'

'A wretched French rascal, *gnä' Fräulein*! A Captain something-or-other. What a fellow . . . I never saw the like. The maids were all screaming and weeping when he presented himself, roaring like a hurricane at them. But now the stupid girls are all giggling and simpering at him. He is chucking them under the chin, and patting their —and patting them, and when Cook came running from the kitchen to see what was amiss, he put his arm about her and kissed her, and now she is as bad as all the rest.'

'He kissed Cook? He is a brave man, then,' Stefanie observed. 'But what can he want?'

'Want? Why, he means to stay here, *gnä' Fräulein*!'

'But that is impossible!' Stefanie cried.

'Of course it is impossible, *gnä' Fräulein*, and don't you think I have told the wretch so? But he will have he is billeted on us, and has an official letter of some sort, addressed to your gracious lady mother, to prove it.'

'Tell him we are exempt from such billets,' said Stefanie firmly.

'Have I not told him? Over and over. But either he can't, or he won't, understand, and he refuses to go away.'

'I see.' Stefanie bit her lip. 'Very well, then, Joachim,' she said briskly. 'Show the captain in here. I'll explain to him myself.'

Joachim backed out grumbling, and could be heard conducting someone towards the door.

'And don't be scuffing the floor with your great boots and knocking the ornaments off all the tables with your sword!' the old man could be heard haranguing the new arrival, who providentially understood not one word of what was being said to him.

Stefanie smiled slightly, but clasped her hands together a little nervously. She glanced quickly about the room, pulled out a chair and sat down facing the door. She had just time to arrange her skirts and assume as formidable and dignified a manner as she could, before the doors were flung open.

Had she been asked just what she expected at that moment, she would have been obliged to admit that it was a wild figure, covered in mud and gore, complete with shako, spurs and sabre and bristling moustachios. It was true that she experienced a moment of pure panic at the glimpse of a tall figure in uniform behind Joachim. 'Cavalry officer . . .' flashed through her mind, like an echo of doom.

However, as it turned out, the fire-breathing, revolution-spreading French wild man who entered the room now, was correctly dressed for calling upon ladies, with his officer's bicorne hat neatly tucked beneath his arm. His uniform was brushed and his Hungarian-style boots highly polished, though admittedly she was not in a mood to appreciate such details. He motioned Joachim to stand out of his way with an imperious flick of his wrist. It was obvious that the old man had succeeded in upsetting him, and the newcomer was certainly not disposed to make any apology for his intrusion. Instead, he made her the briefest of bows, little more than a curt nod, and gave her a look which seemed to indicate he expected some kind of apology from her.

Stefanie, angered by his attitude which seemed to imply that *they* were in the wrong, tilted her chin and said loudly and coldly in French, 'Come in, Captain.'

'Ah!' he said brusquely. 'You speak French. What's this old fool saying?' he nodded towards Joachim.

'What's he calling me?' fumed Joachim, glaring at the officer.

'Leave us,' Stefanie commanded him, finding the furious old man a distraction. She turned her attention back to her visitor. 'You should hardly be surprised at his attitude, Captain, when you force your way into a house in which you are assuredly unwelcome, and to which you have no right of entry. He was attempting to explain to you that this house is exempt from billeting orders. I see you have such an order in your hand. There is some mistake. You must go back to whoever sent you here, and tell them so.'

'Must I indeed?' he returned sarcastically, raising his thick black eyebrows. 'I'm sorry to disappoint you, my dear, but I shall do no such thing. Here I am, and here I stay.'

'You do not!' cried Stefanie angrily, forgetting to be icily cool.

'Tsk, tsk!' He shook a finger at her reprovingly. 'Is that the way to receive a guest? Where are your manners? Why don't you ask me to sit down?' And when she still hesitated, he added, 'Well?' in a minatory tone.

Stefanie took a deep breath. 'Sit down, if you must.'

He put his bicorne on a nearby table and looked round for a chair. Finding a suitable one, he grunted and dragged it forward and had the impertinence to dust the seat before he sat down, displaying a total lack of any embarrassment.

Whilst he did so, Stefanie took the opportunity to study him surreptitiously. It was hard to say how old he was. Perhaps thirty, perhaps a year or two more. But campaigning could have aged him. His face was so tanned by wind and weather that it looked almost leathery, and two long lines ran down either side of his mouth, creasing his lean cheeks. All around his eyes was spun a network of fine wrinkles, perhaps caused by squinting into the dust thrown up by a thousand galloping hooves. He was clean-shaven, but his dark hair had been grown into long side whiskers, touched with early grey. His nose struck her as rather odd. It arched slightly, and seemed to have a disposition to veer to the right, and there was a faint, bony lump on the high bridge. She was later to learn that this was because it had once been badly broken, but now she only thought it loaned a note of cynicism to an imperious yet lively expression, dominated by dark eyes in which gleamed a keen intelligence little would escape.

'And whom have we the honour to welcome into our family home?' she enquired silkily, not to be outdone in the matter of hautiness. Her heart was throbbing like a drum in her breast, almost painfully, but she was determined he should not see her alarm.

'Léon de Vaudry,' he said casually. 'Captain of Dragoons.' He stared at her speculatively. 'Are you the lady of the house?'

'No, my mother is. But she is out.' Stefanie felt herself blushing before that direct appraisal. 'With my sister,' she added.

'*Two* pretty girls?' he observed. 'Then I'm indeed in luck.'

'I doubt it, Captain,' she snapped.

'You speak very good French,' he said approvingly. 'However, I see your education has been neglected in other respects. It would be polite, my dear, to offer me a glass of wine.'

Stefanie seized the little bell on the table by her and rang it with a violence almost fit to break it. Joachim appeared with such alacrity that it was evident he had been lurking behind the door, ready to rescue his young mistress from the dangerous intruder.

'Bring the captain some wine!' she ordered him.

'A good wine,' stipulated their visitor rudely. 'Not some vinegar you keep for the servants. Bring the best.'

'Bring the Tokay,' Stefanie said, giving the captain a look which ought to have shrivelled the soles of his boots.

'I will not,' said Joachim stubbornly. 'That Tokay was sent to your gracious lady mother by your reverend uncle, the Bishop. And it isn't to be poured down the throat of this French devil!'

'Don't argue, Joachim, and bring the Tokay!' snapped Stefanie, releasing some of the pent-up anger she felt towards the Frenchman in the direction of the old man.

'No,' maintained Joachim obstinately. 'Only if your lady mother orders me to, and she's not here.'

'Oh . . . bring the best of something else, then!' Stefanie cried. Struck by a sudden inspiration, she added artfully, 'The French are great wine drinkers, and you surely would not have him think we *have* no good wine here?'

Joachim snorted and withdrew.

'What am I to be given, after all that?' demanded the visitor, who had been following this exchange with close attention and some curiosity.

'I've no idea,' she said vehemently, 'but it won't poison you, whatever it is.'

'Ah?' he said, and unexpectedly gave her a brief grin, deepening the two lines which creased his cheeks. His teeth gleamed very white against his tanned skin, the little lines about his eyes crinkled up attractively and his nose appeared more crooked than ever. He looked completely disreputable.

Stefanie experienced a very curious and inexplicable quivering in the region of the diaphragm, and looked away. It was easy to understand the effect this wretched fellow had had upon the maids. She was grateful that her station in life, and the education she had received, would enable her to resist the obvious physical attraction of a man who, besides being an enemy, had no doubt long ago abandoned the restraints of any accepted moral code with regard to his relationship with the opposite sex.

Suddenly he jumped to his feet and she gave a start of alarm. But he strode past her, across the room to the great double windows and, twisting the wrought iron catch, pulled the inner windows open and inwards, and pushed the outer ones open and out.

'See here,' he said in a sudden change of tone and showing as much enthusiasm as a boy. 'You all have these two sets of windows. I've never seen that before.' He closed the outer windows again carefully and after some deliberation during which he examined the mechanism of the catch, he closed the inner ones too, with a grunt of satisfaction.

'Our winters are very cold . . .' stammered Stefanie, thrown off-balance.

'It's a splendid idea. When I get home again, I shall have some made for my house.'

'You have a house?' Her voice betrayed surprise.

He glanced towards her and said drily, 'Should I not? What do you think I live in, when I'm not soldiering?'

'A stable, to judge by your manners!' she returned angrily.

'Don't lose your temper, *ma belle*, it damages the complexion,' he advised her, unmoved, as if her irritation were no more than the outburst of a petulant child.

He began to stroll around the room, picking up, examining, and putting down the porcelain knicknacks, and studying the paintings, whilst she could only watch him, speechless, and unable to prevent the way in which he seemed to have assumed a kind of right of occupancy, entitling him to do whatever he wished.

By the tiled stove in the corner he said, 'Now, this is something else. We have stoves, but they have little doors, so that one may feed in the fuel. How is it done with these?'

'The doors you may see yourself in the corridor,' said Stefanie aloofly. 'The fuel is fed in by a servant from outside this room. That way, the people in the room need not be disturbed by a servant with a bucket of wood, and the mess which goes with it.'

'No fear of being disturbed by a servant?' he commented with a twitch of an eyebrow. 'Now, that *is* useful!'

'Captain!' she began angrily.

But just then Joachim pushed open the doors and stomped in crossly bearing a silver tray with a glass and a small decanter of wine. Not the Tokay, however, observed Stefanie, annoyed.

'One glass?' asked the visitor, sitting down again. 'You won't drink with me, my dear?'

'Certainly not!' she uttered between gritted teeth.

'A pity.' He tasted the wine and grimaced. 'But wise of you. Your man has brought a wine intended to drive away unwanted visitors. I'm sure you can do better. I drank a better yesterday. We came across the remains of a Russian bivouac. They must have taken to their heels when they heard we were coming, for their officers had left behind half a dozen bottles of a very good wine.'

'Then you should have kept some,' she said coldly, 'and not been obliged to suffer ours!'

'Kept it? That would have seen the bottles broken. A comrade and I drank it for our supper.'

'With your supper? All of it?'

'All of it. *For* our supper, not with our supper. The only other comestible we had was a piece of black bread.'

'Oh, I see . . .' She felt slightly embarrassed. '*Du lieber Gott,*' she thought, 'should we give him something to eat? He's bound to want the best of everything, and if he's been going hungry these last few days . . .'

'Perhaps you would like something to eat now?' she ventured aloud.

'Yes, I should,' was the ungracious reply. 'Tell the old man to bring some bread and cheese.'

Stefanie rang the bell again. 'Send out for some fresh *Semmeln*, Joachim, and bring them with some cheese.'

Whilst they waited, he leaned back in his chair, one heel propped up on the other knee, and surveyed her again, critically. He seemed to miss nothing, from the topmost curl of her hair, to the toes of her shoes, peeping out beneath the hem of her light woollen gown of dark blue.

'Hmn . . .' he said once, but otherwise kept his opinion to himself.

Stefanie was heartily relieved to see Joachim with the food. She watched their visitor devour the rolls and cheese, fascinated. She began to wonder when he *had* eaten properly for the last time. As for the level of the wine, that sank so quickly, it looked as though the decanter had sprung a leak.

'That's better,' he said at last, with some satisfaction, brushing crumbs from his uniform. 'But your Austrian cheeses are not so good as our French ones. Only we French understand how to make a good cheese . . . and good wine,' he added.

'Rubbish, we have excellent wines!' she exploded. 'And there is nothing wrong with our cheese. You ate it fast enough, anyway,' she permitted herself to add sarcastically.

'A man will eat anything when he's hungry. I dined off a dog once.'

'A dog!'

'Just a hind leg . . . that was my share. Grilled,' he added, draining the last of his wine.

'Ugh!' cried Stefanie, aghast. 'How horrible!'

'It wasn't bad, a little tough. And once . . .'

Further revelations were abruptly forestalled by the slam of a door and the sound of Magda's voice crying out excitedly: 'Stefanie! Stefanie! We have seen the French! The carriage was held up by the Kärntnertor, whilst they passed. The Cuirassiers looked so fine with the sun shining on their breastplates. They ride great black Hanoverian horses, which would make the English very cross! Most of the poor horses looked very tired and jaded, though, and some of the infantry marched in rags! And, oh, Stefanie, there were *ladies*! Wives of the officers, riding along beside their husbands! Just imagine, to follow your husband like that on all his campaigns . . . oh!'

Magda burst into the room in her impetuous and child-like way, and stopped short, her face beneath her fur trimmed bonnet a picture of dismay as she saw the unexpected visitor.

'This is Captain de Vaudry, Magda,' said Stefanie woodenly, as the captain scrambled to his feet, looking almost as startled as Magda. 'My sister, Maria-Magdalena, Captain. Mama, may I present the captain to you?'

The Baroness, who had evidently been forewarned by Joachim, entered the room behind Magda, looking unperturbed and mistress of the situation. Stefanie had never admired her mother more.

'I understand you are to be our guest, Captain,' she said graciously.

He bowed in a very correct manner and said, 'Yes,

madame. But only for a day or two. It is not my intention
to inconvenience you.'

'Really?' said the Baroness urbanely. 'I'm sure you
will not. Joachim, show our guest to his room. See
the stove is lit in there immediately. Perhaps the captain would care to take a bath? Tell them to heat
water, Joachim. We shall see you at dinner, Captain.' The Baroness inclined her head in a regal manner
and turned aside to murmur further instructions to
Joachim.

The Frenchman grimaced slightly. 'Thank you,
madame. You are too kind.' He turned to bow politely
to the young ladies. 'Mesdemoiselles . . .'

Magda, who had been watching him, mesmerised,
started back fearfully, as if she had been addressed by
Belial.

Their unpredictable guest could hardly fail to notice
this, and Stefanie saw the displeased look return to his
eyes.

'Are you afraid of me?' he demanded abruptly of
Magda.

'A little, monsieur,' admitted Magda hesitantly, and
turning yet more pale.

'Why?'

'Because you are French, monsieur,' Magda confessed naively.

'That is not a reason to be afraid. You see, your sister
is not!' He glanced sardonically at Stefanie, then,
addressing them both, he went on in a coldly courteous
voice: 'Contrary to rumours you may have heard, the
officers of the French Army are not recruited from a
tribe of savages. We respect the fact that this is an open
city. There is no need to be alarmed at my presence.' His
expression relaxed imperceptibly. 'We do not make war
upon charming young ladies, although we sometimes
make love to them!'

A rosy flush spread into Magda's white cheeks and

Stefanie, seeing his dark eyes glance momentarily at her again, turned her head away quickly.

'I look forward to your company at dinner,' he said to her. 'And I thank you for your welcoming reception . . .'

She opened her mouth to retort, but he was too quick for her, and, with a last flourish of his hat, he had gone.

'I am so sorry, Mama,' said Stefanie, when she had briefly summarised what had happened earlier for her mother and sister. 'He would not go away, though I tried to explain his billet was a mistake. He will regale you at dinner with tales of having dined on a dog, and similar stories, and will find fault with every dish.'

'I doubt it,' said the Baroness calmly, pulling off her gloves. 'He seems a presentable young man and, I perceive, a gentleman. I am surprised there are any still left in France since the lamentable revolution. I'm sure he knows how to behave at the dinner table.'

Stefanie stared at her in some surprise.

'My dears,' said her mother, 'you must pay careful attention to what I say now. Captain de Vaudry is our guest. He will be treated as any guest in this house, that is to say with the greatest courtesy. He shall have every necessary comfort, and we shall be pleasant to him. However, we shall have to mind our tongues. You, Magda, my dear, are inclined to prattle in a thoughtless manner. And you, Stefanie, are sometimes inclined to let your temper lead your tongue. Either of these situations could be disastrous. The captain appears a quick-witted young man and would not fail to seize on any small item of information gleaned from indiscreet conversation on our part.'

'Then we must let him stay here?' Stefanie asked with a leaden heart. 'We can surely obtain his removal. Could not Hofrat von Letzberg make representations to the French . . .'

'We should but needlessly offend the captain, and the French too. We might even see him replaced by some-one more objectionable. For all Vienna is an "open" city, it is very much an occupied one. For the moment, at least, the French are our masters. It would be unwise to offend them. Captain de Vaudry will respond in kind, I am sure, to civil treatment. But should we persist in being uncivil to him, we might see a side to the Captain's character which would be highly disagreeable for us.'

'So he may do as he pleases, and we may do nothing?' cried Stefanie.

'I fear so, my dear.' The Baroness sighed and left the room.

'Oh no,' said Stefanie quietly to Magda, 'the Captain will not make use of us, treating our house as a common inn! He will be sorry he ever forced his unwelcome company upon us. He will rue the day, I promise you, he ever set foot in this house!'

CHAPTER
THREE

WHAT was required now, thought Stefanie, brushing vigorously at her shining corn-gold hair, was a strategy as carefully planned as any of Bonaparte's. To be revenged on the captain for the insult done her family by his very presence in its midst, she must single out some weakness in her foe. She did not know Captain Léon de Vaudry well, it was true. But she could guess at *one* weakness.

She flung open the doors of the great walnut wardrobe which housed her gowns and Magda's, and surveyed the serried ranks critically. Now, which?

Magda, seated by the dressing table and staring musingly at her own pretty and serious reflection, was twisting one of her dark curls around her forefinger. It was a childhood habit she had never lost and it indicated deep thought.

'He's very handsome,' she said, 'in a *different* sort of way.'

Stefanie was pulling out the gowns energetically from the wardrobe, one after the other, and flinging the rejected ones down on the bed.

'Blue is too ordinary,' she muttered, 'and pink too insipid.'

'His nose is crooked, didn't you notice?' Magda pushed her own delicate retroussé nose to one side and gave a little giggle at the resulting reflection in the mirror.

'Lavender might be possible . . .' from Stephanie, holding a lavender silk against her and turning from side

33

to side before the cheval glass. Her loose golden hair swung to and fro.

'I don't think he means to be frightening,' gave Magda as her opinion now.

'What?' Stefanie glanced at her sister. 'Doesn't he *just*! Be frank, Magda, does crimson make me look fat?'

'Red dresses always make me think of lobsters,' said Magda devastatingly.

Stefanie tossed the crimson gown aside. 'Then that's not for me.'

'Why are you worrying so much about what to wear at dinner?' asked Magda curiously.

'I mean to make an impression. Of course, white would be the most fashionable . . .' Stefanie considered. 'But too . . . too virginal! I want to look a woman of the world.'

'Do you?' asked Magda doubtfully. 'Mama says it is a mistake for a young girl to pretend to be more sophisticated than she is. The wrong men will kiss you!' added Magda, placing her own practical interpretation on her mother's warning words.

'He may try . . .' said Stefanie with an amused smile.

Magda swung round on her stool. 'Stefanie! You can't want Captain de Vaudry to try and kiss you? Or *do* you? I thought you found him rude and overbearing.'

Stefanie turned from her search in the wardrobe, an odd glitter in her beautiful eyes. 'Listen to me, Magda my precious. *That man* has invited himself into our house, where he will drink our wine and eat our food and generally make use of our hospitality, whether we wish it or not. He may have everything he wishes—or so he thinks! He need but snap his fingers and we shall run to do his bidding and supply his wants. But we are perhaps not so powerless against him as may seem. Our captain is not invulnerable, though he has a very high opinion of himself, has Captain de Vaudry! He fancies himself a ladies' man, too, I am sure, as do all the French. And *that* is his Achilles' heel—in his self-esteem! There is where he may be wounded, and we may be revenged! For there is one thing I am determined he shall want, truly want, and find he *cannot* have. And that is me! I am going to make Captain de Vaudry fall in love with me. And when he has, I shall reject him utterly, and there will be nothing he can do about it!'

'Oh, Stefanie,' Magda whispered. 'You mustn't. You don't know what he might do. He isn't like other men of our acquaintance . . .'

'Oh, yes, he is,' said Stefanie serenely. 'In *that* way he is like *all* other men!' She dived triumphantly into the depths of the wardrobe and emerged clasping a striking gown of black satin with an overskirt of fine Hungarian lace. 'The very thing! Have you your scissors, Magda?'

'In my embroidery box,' said Magda obediently, producing the scissors. 'Stefanie, what are you doing?'

Her sister was snipping vigorously at the trim around the low square neckline of the black dress. 'Unpicking this trim to make the neck lower. More *décolleté*, you know. That will take the Captain's mind from our "inferior" wines and "insipid" cheeses, and our indiscreet conversation!'

'By fixing his attention on your indiscreet necklines, I suppose?' said Magda primly. 'You won't do it. You wouldn't dare.'

'I shall!'

Mitzi, the Baroness' personal maid, came into the room and asked: 'You wished me to dress your hair, *gnädiges Fräulein*?'

'Yes, please, Mitzi. Lots of curls and nice, teasing little fronds over the ears. Magda, dear, you won't mind if I borrow a little of your best cologne water?'

When, at last, she was ready to her own satisfaction, Stefanie presented herself before the openly dismayed Magda, and demanded impatiently: 'Well? How do I look?'

'You . . . you look lovely, Stefanie,' said Magda in an awed little voice. 'You look quite beautiful. I've never seen you look more enchanting. But, oh, Stefanie, I do think that you're being horribly indiscreet!'

'Don't worry, it is the captain who will be indiscreet!' Stefanie promised her, giving a little tug to the bodice of the black satin so that it revealed a further half inch of white bosom.

'Oh, Stefanie, dearest, don't!' cried poor Magda, bursting into tears. 'I do think you are taking such a dreadful risk. Suppose you are making a terrible mistake?'

'Nonsense!' said Stefanie determinedly. 'I know exactly what I am doing.'

She was certainly successful enough in making an impression, for he stared at her very hard when she entered and then ran an appreciative eye over her graceful figure. But it was not quite as she had thought it would be, somehow. For all her earlier confidence before Magda, she felt, before him, distressingly naked. To be sure, she was decent . . . but hardly modest. To have his eyes actually resting on that bold neckline, sent a pink flush creeping up her throat, especially as his glance was accompanied not only by a look of admiration, but by a quizzical lift of his black eyebrows and the very faintest amused twitch at the corners of his mouth.

'Very elegant, mademoiselle,' he said at last. 'You look *almost* fashionable enough for a Parisian salon.'

'What do you mean, *almost*?' demanded Stefanie, forgetting for the moment that she was the cool seductress.

'You lack a little of that Parisian *chic*, but you do very well,' was the condescending reply.

'I do very . . .! I do very well for what, may I ask?'

'Why, to take into dinner,' he said. 'May I offer you my arm, mademoiselle?' He bowed most respectfully, perhaps a little too respectfully, as he made this request, and there was an enigmatic look in the dark eyes.

Her instinct was to give a biting reply, for she had the most distinct impression she was being mocked, but she remembered the challenge she had set herself and, smiling archly, replied, 'Then let us go in, Captain!' She placed her hand on his sleeve.

'They look very fine together,' whispered Magda to her mother in a mixture of admiration and despair.

'Yes,' said the Baroness calmly. 'He is a very handsome man. Also the breaker of a score of hearts, I don't doubt, and several reputations.'

'Oh, Mama,' begged Magda, 'please tell Stefanie that!'

The Baroness gave a slightly weary smile. 'My dear child, Stefanie is woman enough to know it already.'

'She cannot, or she would not behave as she is!'

'Would she not? I never yet met a woman who was deterred by a man's reputation,' the Baroness said. 'I fear my poor daughter knows very little about men . . . but is about to learn something.'

'You are not afraid for her?' asked Magda, bewildered. 'I'm terrified.'

'I have confidence in Stefanie, if that is what you mean,' said the Baroness severely. 'She may lose her heart, but she will not lose her head.'

Early November twilight had already necessitated the lighting of the candles on the small, round table which the Baroness had ordered to be set, so that they might be more informal. Stefanie, seething gently whilst smiling winsomely outwardly, observed that their guest, besides having bathed and shaved, had somehow acquired some starched linen, as the high points of his white chemise above the round collar of his *surtout*, bore witness. How he had managed this sartorial *tour-de-force* when he had spent the last few weeks on campaign, she had no idea. But she did not doubt he was a resourceful fellow, besides a thorough rogue. Grudgingly, she admitted to herself that he looked very dashing, in a hard-bitten sort of way. But not a man to trifle with, and she began to wonder uneasily whether ingenuous Magda had not been more astute than she in judging the newcomer. He *was* different from the other men of her narrow social circle. At least she could be sure of them, and she was very far from feeling she could be sure of him. She must be careful, it would be only too easy to become the victim, and not the victor, in the little game she had undertaken to play.

Somewhat to her surprise, her mother was proved correct almost immediately in one respect. Far from criticising the dishes set before him, he showed great appreciation and some considerable discernment. He was remarkably curious to know the culinary details of everything.

'What is this sauce? What do you call it?' he demanded.

'That is what we call gipsy sauce, or cooked gipsy fashion,' the Baroness told him.

'Indeed? Your gipsies must eat better than ours. What spice gives this red colour and this flavour?'

'Paprika.'

'I don't know it. Show me some,' he ordered next.

Unperturbed, the Baroness signalled to Joachim and a small dish was duly brought containing a tablespoon of paprika pepper and set before him.

'I shall send some to my mother,' he said unexpectedly. 'She is always curious to try something new in the kitchen.'

'Then you should know that there are two kinds, the *edelsüss* and the *edelscharf*,' the Baroness said. 'I shall have Cook make up a packet of each for your mother.'

He looked up and saw Stefanie was staring at him in apparent amazement.

'What is the matter?' he asked brusquely. 'I know you don't think I could own a house. Do you think I could not have a mother either? Perhaps you think I arrived in this world booted and spurred, to the accompaniment of a clap of thunder and infernal laughter?'

'You tease my daughter, Captain!' said the Baroness with a smile.

Stefanie flushed hotly. 'You may amuse yourself, Captain, as you wish,' she said.

Joachim was pouring out the wine. There was still no sign of the Tokay, which Joachim was evidently determined to preserve with his life, if need be.

'I trust you will like this wine, Captain,' said the Baroness. 'It is from the Burgenland, where we own a small vineyard. We are so far pleased with our own wine as to offer it to our guests.'

'You are rightly proud,' he said, adding, 'my family owns a vineyard, near to Epernay.'

So he was the son of country landowners. Her mother was a shrewd judge of people, Stefanie thought. She herself would have put the captain down as an adventurer, a *sans-culotte* who had risen from the ranks. Her mother was more perceptive, for de Vaudry was a fairly distinguished sort of name, after all. A sudden horrifying thought struck Stefanie. He could even . . .

But her mother was still ahead of her.

'I think it possible, Captain,' she said, 'that you have some other title, apart from your military one.'

'I am Count de Vaudry,' he admitted. 'But the title carries little with it. We lost most of our property in 1789, and what is left brings in only a modest income. I am obliged to go soldiering, as you see. To have a title is now fashionable again in France,' he added. 'But I cannot hope mine will make my career. I suppose,' he concluded, 'that I am something of a soldier of fortune.'

'Why did you not tell me this?' Stefanie demanded angrily.

'It would have made you pleased to see me, would it?' he asked, rather insultingly.

'It might have saved some embarrassment,' she said accusingly.

'Were you embarrassed? I had not realised it,' he replied consolingly.

'No, I was not!' she raged at him.

'Nor was I. Who was, then?'

'You mean to be as awkward as possible,' cried Stefanie, exasperated at last.

'No, I don't. You do!' he retaliated.

'Ah . . .' murmured the Baroness, a gleam in her fine eyes.

'I did not tell you,' he continued to Stefanie, 'because I did not wish you to feel obliged to offer me your hospitality.'

'But you claim our hospitality anyway!'

'Yes. But I did not oblige you to offer it,' he reminded her.

Stefanie felt she had lost this argument and fell silent. Not for long, however.

Picking up his glass of wine, he pushed back his chair, stood up and, raising his glass on high, proposed in a loud firm voice, 'The Emperor!'

'The Emperor Franz!' cried Magda loyally.

'No,' he corrected politely. '*The* Emperor!'

'He means Napoleon,' said Stefanie crossly, 'who has made himself an emperor, which is nonsense.'

'Stefanie . . .!' warned her mother sharply, but it was too late.

Their guest set down his glass and said very coolly, 'You think him unworthy, perhaps?'

Stefanie, not a little alarmed by the very hard look in his eyes and the set of his mouth, said defensively, 'One cannot make oneself Emperor. Bonaparte has no claim to such a title.'

'He needs no claim. He has won it for himself. When

your Emperor Franz, or the Czar either, come to that, has done as much to earn his title as Napoleon has done to earn his, then either or both of them may challenge his right to it, but not before.'

'His victories on the battlefield have given it to him, then?' she demanded.

'Winner takes all, mademoiselle,' he said softly, but in a tone of voice which frightened her very much.

'I propose,' said the Baroness calmly, 'that we each toast "the Emperor". Whom we mean by that, we shall each keep to ourselves.'

He hesitated, then picked up his glass again. 'Very well. I to my emperor. You to yours.'

They drank the toast accordingly. Afterwards, there was an awkward silence, then the Baroness left the table and Stefanie and Magda followed her out of the room. He stood, watching them go. When they had left, he sat down again and glanced at Joachim, who was standing quietly a little to one side of him.

'Bring me your brandy,' he ordered abruptly. 'And don't pretend not to understand me.'

'I'll bring it,' muttered Joachim beneath his breath. 'But you'll not get your rogue's hands on our Tokay, you hound of hell. I'll pour it into the gutters first.'

Stefanie had made an excuse to leave her mother and sister and go to the room she shared with Magda. She wanted to sit quietly for a few moments and gather her composure. There was something very frightening about Captain de Vaudry, or *monsieur le capitaine comte* de Vaudry! she thought angrily. Oddly enough, it was not when he shouted and demanded that he was alarming. It was when he was at his most quiet, and then he was terrifying. However, although she had begun to suspect she had made a serious mistake, she was not quite yet ready to abandon her plans.

At last, reluctantly, she made her way back towards

the drawing room from which she could hear Magda's voice. But, at the final moment, her nerve failed her, and she turned aside into the—as she thought it—deserted dining room.

He was still there, standing before one of the portraits, a glass of brandy in his hand. All the candles had been extinguished except for two which burned on a sidetable, illuminating the portrait which hung on the wall above them. The extinguished candles still smouldered, filling the air with the scent of hot wax. The dusky golden glow from the remaining two encapsuled him, and threw flickering shadows onto his face, emphasising and distorting the strong features. He looked to her almost as if he were some pagan war god, who had emerged from the mists of antiquity to don Napoleonic uniform, and inspire mere mortals with a supernatural urge to strive for Death or Glory.

'Or Glory through Death,' she thought soberly. 'He would lay down his life for his Emperor and the imperial standards, and count it an honour. What kind of men are these?'

She was almost startled when he spoke.

'This is your mother,' he said without preamble, and indicating the portrait with a gesture of the brandy glass.

'Yes, painted shortly before her marriage.' Stefanie came to stand a little way away from him in the gloom beyond the ring of candlelight, afraid to step into the intimacy of that golden circle, as though, once in it, she could never escape. She rested a hand on a convenient chairback, seeking a reassuring touch, if only that of an inanimate but familiar object.

'So she would have been about the same age as you are now?'

'Yes,' Stefanie said, barely audibly.

'She has kept her looks well,' he said. 'And I see a resemblance between her and you in this portrait.'

'So people say,' Stefanie agreed, making a determined effort to rally herself and reassume the role she had undertaken for that evening. 'I am said to take after my mother, and Magda after our father. I am fair, she is dark.'

'A family of very beautiful women,' he remarked.

'You are gallant, Captain,' she said archly. He had chosen to conceal his title from her, and she was determined, therefore, to ignore it. He had introduced himself as simply 'Captain'—and so he would remain for her. 'We are honoured by your compliments.'

He turned to face her, a somewhat cynical expression on his face. 'Don't say you don't know you are beautiful,' he said. 'I'm sure you do. Isn't that what this,' he indicated the black satin, 'is all about? I might even suspect it is for my benefit that you have taken such pains to make yourself so desirable. I say this without conceit, since I am the only man present. You have been more than successful. You are enchanting . . . and there is no reason why a soldier's heart should be less susceptible than any other man's.'

So he had not been deceived. He had guessed her little scheme from the very outset. Humiliated, she said in a low angry voice, 'You flatter yourself. Do you think I care for your approval? Were you not a guest in this house, then I should have told you to your face that you are arrogant, conceited and impertinent! You have forgotten your manners amongst men and horses, and no longer know how to behave in the presence of women of good family. Save your gallantries for the maidservants, who will no doubt appreciate them more!'

'Well-born lady or maidservant,' he said, setting down his brandy glass deliberately. 'What makes you think there is so much difference?'

She saw something in his eyes then which sent signals of alarm racing up and down her spine. What remained of her earlier desire to be an enchantress, a 'woman of the world', evaporated quickly, and she was only aware that she was alone with this man whose interest she had sought, only too successfully, to arouse. She had set in train a physical reaction which was beyond her experience, and which she did not know how to reverse. Nothing which had gone before had frightened her so much as this. For a second she had glimpsed in his face something almost primitive and animal, as old as time, obscured but not eradicated by the superficialities of civilisation. She started back, but with a sudden step towards her, he seized her shoulders in a grip of steel. She gave a smothered cry, as, bending his head, he grasped her blonde curls roughly, forcing her face up to his, so that their lips met in an encounter the violence of which both terrified and aroused her.

She began to struggle in his arms, knowing that it was useless, not only because he was very strong, but because in a strange and incomprehensible way her own body conspired with him against her will. The pressure of his mouth was conjuring up a response from deep within her which she could not ignore, and knew he must sense, too.

'I told you,' he whispered in her ear. 'Winner takes all!'

'No!' With a strength born of desperation, she managed to free her right arm and pushed the palm of her hand against his face with all the force at her command. He uttered an exclamation in French which she did not recognise—no doubt because it was not one commonly used in the presence of ladies—and, still clasping her tightly about the waist with one arm, he flung out the other to seize hold of her raised wrist, and wrenched her hand violently away from his face so that she gasped in pain.

'So now you mean to scratch my eyes out, do you?' he demanded in a low, dangerous tone. 'You blow hot and cold, mademoiselle. I advise you not to play such games with me! You've signalled a clear enough invitation to me all evening—you can hardly have thought I would refuse it? Well, I do not refuse it, and *you* will not refuse me, now!'

'I am not playing any game, not now. Let go of me, please!' she whispered in a pleading voice. 'I *was* pretending, and I'm sorry. But I'm not pretending now!' She was shaking from head to toe. Her eyes, fixed on his angry face, were dilated with fear, and the colour had drained from her cheeks, leaving them a porcelain whiteness.

He made no reply as he stared down into her face. Then the anger faded from his eyes to be replaced by an expression less easy to interpret. Slowly, he stretched out his hand to the black satin which had been dragged from one shoulder as she had wrenched her arm free. He bowed his head to kiss the bare white skin lightly, and the touch of his lips, in contrast so gentle now, seemed to burn into the flesh.

'You have a skin like the first snow of winter,' he said softly. Then, with a slightly wry smile, he carefully adjusted the gown. 'We must have you looking decent, *ma chère*,' he observed in his former dry manner. 'I don't want to be accused of attempting rape. I think your Frau Mama awaits us. Come!' He held out his hand.

She backed away from him, shaking her head. 'I . . . can't . . .'

'Do as I say,' he said in that quiet voice which was not to be refused.

Unable to speak, she stretched out her trembling hand to his. As she felt his strong fingers close on hers, some force seemed to communicate itself between them, like one of those frightening and beautiful flashes of light she had once seen demonstrated at a lecture on the unexplored power of something called electricity. In that moment she knew that nothing could ever be the same again, and that no man's touch could ever equal this man's. A soldier, a stranger, an enemy—he had taken possession of the Snowmaiden's heart with that one brutal kiss and had made it his for ever. Unresistingly, she allowed him to lead her to rejoin the others.

CHAPTER
FOUR

THEY did not see their guest the whole of the following morning and Stefanie, for one, was heartily glad of it. She dreaded his appearance. Every step outside the door caused her to look up guiltily. She opened a book and tried to read, but the lettering danced before her eyes. If he had kissed her, then she could only blame herself, and she could not think of the whole episode without feelings of shame. Never would she be able to forget the clasp of those strong arms and the pressure of that mouth on hers, and that look in his eyes. Most of all, she recalled that look of undisguised desire, a look so different to the admiring but courteous glances of the young officers who frequented her mother's parties.

'You're very flushed, Stefanie,' remarked her mother. 'Don't sit so near to the stove.'

Stefanie moved her chair and opened the door again. How to receive him when he did come? To ignore him would be impossible, just as to ignore what had happened the previous evening would be both impractical and foolish. She was obliged to accept that she had played with fire, and had burnt her fingers. As to her own feelings . . . Stefanie resolutely thrust those into the recesses of her mind where they lurked banished, but by no means forgotten.

She decided that outwardly she would be polite, cool and gracious to the Captain, just as her mother was. But she would keep him firmly in his place, and let him know, if he attempted any familiarity, that he was not to presume upon the mistakes of one evening. All this, she was miserably aware, might not be so easy to put into practice, excellent though it was in theory.

'You've been reading that page for half an hour,' whispered Magda. 'It must be very interesting!'

He returned at last in the early afternoon with a suggestion that he be allowed to escort them on a stroll through the city.

'I should like to view this Vienna of yours, since I have the opportunity, and may not have it for long, or indeed, ever again.'

'I shall not accompany you, Monsieur de Vaudry,' said the Baroness. 'But as the day is not unpleasant for the time of year, I have no objection to my daughters walking around the city ramparts with you.'

With a sinking heart, Stefanie said heroically, 'It will take us about an hour, if you walk at our pace. It is a favourite stroll of the Viennese.'

In fact, she would not be sorry to be out in the fresh air. She had slept badly, and indoors the atmosphere within the tightly sealed rooms was heavy and stuffy from the heat of the wood-burning tiled stoves. Her head ached and she felt dull and listless. Besides, perhaps it would be easier to place matters between them on a proper footing, outside of the house.

The previous month, October, had seen snow. But since then the weather had been milder than usual for the time of year.

'Even the elements favour Napoleon's advance,' Hofrat von Letzberg had observed drily.

Today it was cold and crisp, but sunny, and even atop the ramparts there was no more than a moderate breeze. They proceeded along sedately, the two girls placed one either side of their gallant escort and, as Magda was struck dumb by nerves, the burden of the conversation fell on Stefanie.

'You are not cold?' he asked her, his eyes resting on her pale face.

She felt his gaze, but could not return it. 'No, I was only thinking, how many French uniforms are to be seen.'

He began to tell her the names of the different regiments, pointing out especially the uniforms of the Imperial Guard. 'Although most of those gentlemen,' he added casually, 'are at Schönbrunn, surrounding the Emperor.'

He always referréd to Napoleon as 'the Emperor', and Stefanie knew better now than to dispute the title Bonaparte had conferred upon himself. But she thought she detected a note of sarcasm in his reference to the Guard.

'One hears,' she said, 'that they are the finest troops in the world. They look magnificent.'

'Oh, yes. They are hand-picked. One would be pleased to see them all in action.' He did not elaborate on this obscure remark, but went on, 'What a strange sort of place your city is. Half of it is squashed inside the ramparts, a rabbit warren of streets and alleys, none of them with any pavements for wretches like us who must walk. Fine mansions, tenements, shops, churches, coffee houses and public ballrooms, are all jumbled together gasping for air. Then, beyond the city walls comes this great empty space—'

'The *glacis*,' Magda contributed, breaking her silence at last. 'No one is allowed to build there.'

'But beyond it the palaces and mansions begin again. From up here we can see them clearly.' He pointed out to the distant palaces beyond the *glacis*. 'What you should do, when peace comes, is to knock down these venerable ramparts and build a great boulevard, so that the outer and inner cities may grow together.'

'Knock down Vienna's walls?' cried Stefanie, scandalised. 'The Viennese would be sorry to see them go. Besides, we need them.'

'To keep out the French?' he asked, giving her a sideways glance and a little grin. 'City walls are no match for modern artillery.'

'You did not need your artillery to breach them *this* time,' Stefanie told him, 'for we were betrayed into your hands. But next time it may be different! If our Russian allies had stood by us . . .'

'I pray there may not be a next time,' Magda interrupted her frankly. 'I pray for peace.'

'May your prayers be answered, mademoiselle. I dare say they will be, eventually. But not before a great deal of blood has been spilt. Besides, what should I do in peacetime? Sit at Epernay and watch the grapes ripen on the vines? A Dragoon is a fighting machine. He is trained to fight on horseback or on foot. He is a creature of war. Take away the scenes of carnage where he flourishes, and he looses his *raison d'être*, he becomes a wraith.'

'I do not know,' Stefanie said energetically, 'whether you speak as a philosopher or as an animal!'

'I speak as a soldier. He is both. And speaking of soldiers, you are too hard on your Russian allies, mademoiselle Stefanie. Kutuzov is an old, one-eyed fox. He retreats so that he may fight again another day. With every league he leads us onwards, further from France, and nearer to his Russian reinforcements. Over there—' He pointed suddenly eastwards. 'Over there he will make his stand and we shall not take him so easily as we took your Austrian army at Ulm.'

'You despise our Austrian army, no doubt?' said Stefanie stiffly.

'By no means. The Austrian is always a gallant and worthy adversary. Properly led—'

'Our officers are very fine and brave!' cried Magda indignantly.

'And represent our first families,' added Stefanie rashly.

'Oho! Of course! If a man may put *von und zu* before his name, what other qualifications does he need? Well, *I* have a title, and an old and honourable one, but the only honours I would wish, are honours I have won! See here, my dears, I know your Austrian officers have courage, for I've seen it for myself. But they cannot withstand us. No one can. Destiny is for us! Nothing can stop us now.' His voice gained more and more enthusiasm as he spoke and his saturine features glowed. The years seemed to drop away, softening the hard lines and rendering his face boyish in its victorious optimism. 'The Emperor's star is in the ascendant, and as he rises, as he must, so he takes France with him!'

The conviction in his voice silenced both girls for a moment. Then Stefanie rallied and objected: 'I do not believe it. You have said yourself that the Russians will not retreat for ever, nor will what is left of our Austrian army. Together—'

'Together you may thrash us soundly? Perhaps.'

'Oh, stop!' cried Magda suddenly in tones of great distress. 'Stop talking about *fighting*. It means people being killed!'

'Ah!' he said. 'Your little sister has a lover amongst the Austrian officers. Come now, admit it, *ma petite*.'

'Yes,' muttered Magda in a muffled voice.

'A fine young fellow, I'm sure. What is the name of this paragon?'

'Andreas von Letzberg,' Magda said, tears welling up into her eyes.

'Don't weep for your "faithful Hussar", my pretty. He's not doing any fighting just now. *We're* all here! I promise you, should I see a particularly handsome and worthy young man charging at me, sabre drawn, I shall yell, "Are you von Letzberg, by any chance? If so, I shall try and avoid killing you".'

'Oh!' wailed Magda.

'Be quiet, Captain!' stormed Stefanie. 'Can't you see how afraid she is for Andreas?'

'Take heart,' he said consolingly. '*He* may kill *me*!'

'I don't want you to kill him, or him to kill you! I don't want anyone to kill anybody!' cried Magda in great distress and agitation. 'I want you to go home to your vineyards and Andreas to come home to me!' She ran away from them, slowing down some yards ahead to walk by herself.

'Now you see what you have done?' Stefanie exclaimed angrily. 'Why must you upset everybody? It is all very well for you. I suppose you fear nothing and nobody, and scorn all timorous hearts.'

He stopped and turned to look down into her face. His own was suddenly very sober. The dark eyes fixed her with a look she could not quite comprehend, full of some secret pain, some old memory, old nightmares perhaps, which haunted him still. Then he began to walk on quickly so that she had difficulty in keeping up with him. With his eyes fixed ahead, he said:

'Only an idiot or a liar looks you in the eye and swears he was never afraid. What man isn't afraid when he sees the mouth of the guns turned towards his square and the gunners ramming home the shot which will perhaps take his head off? Every soldier has seen a whole line of his fellows reduced to shattered, bleeding remnants by grapeshot, has seen a whole team of horses pulling an artillery piece killed at one blast. He has heard men and horses scream in agony. Of course he knows what fear is. But he learns to live with it. After a while, he becomes accustomed to it. It is like an inconvenient companion who will not go away and so must be tolerated and checked if he becomes too troublesome. But when the fighting is hand to hand, why, then, frankly, you have no time to be afraid. You see this battered nose of mine? It was smashed by the butt of a carbine at Marengo, by a fellow who was out of ammuniton, and knew he must die. But his thoughts were less of fear, than of vengeance. He knew I must kill him, but he meant to maim me first.'

'And did you kill him?' she asked quietly.

'I . . . or someone else . . . what does it matter?' he replied moodily, after a pause. Then he fell silent again, lost in some private reverie.

'Tell me,' she said, curious to know more about him, 'tell me something about before . . . before you were a Dragoon.'

'I have forgotten there was ever such a time.' He frowned as if making a difficult recollection. 'If there was, it seems a thousand years ago.' After a moment, he went on, 'What I remember best is, when I was still young, little more than a boy, though fancying myself a man! It was in 1793, at the onset of the Terror in France. They came one night to our house to arrest my father. We were all got out of bed. The drums were beating, and in the torchlight I could see the hostile faces of the ruffians sent from the local Committee of Public Safety, and I was near to tears. My father asked me, what was the matter. I said, "I am afraid." He said, "We are all afraid. The important thing is not to show it. Never let them see it." Those were the last words he spoke to me before he was led away.'

'What happened to him?' Stefanie asked in a whisper.

'My father? He went to the guillotine, along with so many others. It was a common enough story in those days.'

'Captain,' she asked suddenly, 'may I ask how old you are?'

He flashed his disreputable grin at her. 'You flatter me, mademoiselle, by this display of interest. I am twenty-seven.'

'So young?' she said seriously. 'I thought you some years older.'

'Alas, now you do not flatter me. I look old and

decrepit, do I? Oh, well, perhaps I have grown old quickly. Perhaps I grew up in that one night when they came for my father. After that, I was certainly never a child again.'

It was as if some barrier had been temporarily removed between them. For a brief moment, the veil of arrogance and cynical humour had been drawn aside, and she glimpsed the man behind the uniform. She could not feel she understood him, this determined, confident, clever, ruthless, and yet, she was beginning to suspect, inwardly lonely man, who walked beside her. But one thing was clear to her. He had come into her sheltered, comfortable, happy world, from a world of heroism and barbarity, noble self-sacrifice and foul atrocity which she could never understand and, please God, would never have to face.

Impulsively, she touched his hand and said, 'If I have wronged you, I am sorry. These are things of which I know nothing. Whatever you are, your life has made you that. My life has been very sheltered. I am perhaps very ignorant.'

He squeezed her fingers slightly in his firm grip which sent a tremor running through her whole body, and replied, 'No, no. You are an intelligent, spirited and beautiful woman, and I am a person who has had all that was ever fine in me crushed. And too many casual affairs of the heart—no! No, that is untrue. The heart never entered into it. Too many amusements of the flesh, perhaps, to appreciate the challenge of any relationship worth seeking and having . . .'

'Please don't . . .' she whispered, her heart pounding, and trying to pull her hand from his.

'Don't be afraid,' he said. 'You, who are so bold! What is it you fear, eh?' He smiled and, lifting her hand, gently kissed her gloved fingers before releasing her.

'Not long after my father's death, a few months,' he went on with his story, 'Dragoons were quartered in our village on their way to the Low Countries. I presented myself before their commanding officer and when they moved out, I went with them.'

'Your poor mother. To lose you so soon after losing your father. Did she not object?'

'She knew nothing of it, poor soul, till I was far away. But she was a sensible woman. She knew I was safer with the Dragoons than at home, in such times. Though she feared the Dragoons rough company for her boy! They were rough, certainly, but good fellows. They knew I was a *ci-devant*, a cursed *aristo*, and therefore suspect, but they said nothing of it, and even protected me when the commissions of enquiry came round, Fouquier-Tinville's head-hunters! So I survived, and here I am!' he concluded quite cheerfully. 'A captain of horse in receipt of eighteen hundred *livres* a year, on which I am supposed to maintain myself and the three horses required of me by regulations. Though I am down to two horses. One beast drowned when we crossed the river Enns. You don't know where I can get another, I suppose?'

'I wish I had known some of this when you came to the house,' said Stefanie thoughtfully. 'I might have overlooked your very rude behaviour. You behaved very badly, Captain, when you presented yourself yesterday.'

'So did you. You have no idea how much trouble I took dressing for that first call. I had to go and unearth a little Austrian tailor to repair and press my walking out dress, and borrow some clean linen from a comrade, for I did not want to terrify you by bursting in with sabre and helmet. I consider I was very badly received, firstly by the servants, and then by you.'

'I did not notice your reception discouraged you! And Joachim said you kissed the maids, even Cook!'

'I've always found it the best way to stop a woman screeching,' was the confident reply. 'Generally they don't mind, not so much as they say they do, anyway.'

He glanced wickedly at her. 'Is the cook the large lady with the moustache? My word, she'd make a Dragoon!'

Despite herself, Stefanie burst into laughter.

'You know,' he said, smiling down at her, 'that is the first time I have heard you laugh, really laugh. Why don't you laugh more often? It is an enchanting laugh, sweet as a bell.'

'Goodness, Captain, do stop! I shall never laugh again.'

'But so much nicer than the awful scowls which greeted me yesterday as you ordered me back whence I came—which you obviously thought was from the Infernal Regions. You were determined I was a ruffian, so why not behave like one? And as for the even worse coy simpers directed at me later over the dinner table—'

'Stop, and I do mean *stop*!' cried Stefanie in an agony. 'Never speak of that, never! Surely you can understand that I made a foolish mistake, and I should like it forgotten!'

'As you wish, *ma belle*. But *I* haven't forgotten, nor what followed . . .'

'Neither have I,' thought Stefanie wretchedly. 'I never shall.'

They had caught up with Magda, who was leaning over the ramparts, staring out across the *glacis*, and holding onto her fur-trimmed bonnet, as a means of hiding her face from passers-by.

'Come now, you are angry with me,' he said to her quite kindly.

'No,' Magda told him. 'You didn't do it on purpose.'

'You have a noble heart, *ma chère petite*. May young von Letzberg prove worthy of it. Here, take my arm, that's better. Mademoiselle Stefanie, where are you? There! How could a man be better off than with two such enchanting damsels, one on either arm? Now, let's see, I shall make you laugh. Are you listening, little Magda? I shall tell you a story about a Hungarian officer.'

'Which Hungarian officer?' asked Magda innocently.

'Oh, any Hungarian officer. I dare say one is worth another. This is an amusing story, dear young lady, a joke, if you will. Don't spoil it by being so pedantic.'

'What sort of amusing story?' asked Stefanie suspiciously, for there was an impish look of mischief in his eye which she mistrusted profoundly.

'It's generally thought to be a very good one, though I never had to tell it to such a difficult audience. Will you be quiet? Now, this Hungarian officer had made the acquaintance of a young woman, as these things go, and after he—'

'Captain de Vaudry!' interrupted Stefanie vigorously. 'My sister is only seventeen! I do not know what kind of story you propose telling her—and me—but I suspect it is highly unsuitable, and I can't imagine why you should think it would make her laugh, even if she understood it, which is unlikely! I suggest you keep your licentious narratives for the ears of *vivandières* and camp followers!'

'Oh, I forgot,' he said insolently. 'I have heard of your Austrian arch-duchesses, who are so carefully brought up that their governesses set to work and cut all suggestive references out of books before their charges read them, and before whom all unsuitable paintings and statues are veiled! Were *you* brought up with such admirable prudence? After yesterday evening, I find it hard to believe!'

'Magda, come!' commanded Stefanie imperiously, trembling with anger. 'My sister and I will go down these steps and home. We do not require you to escort us. You, Captain, I am sure, can find your way back alone. Provided, of course, you don't meet any of those agreeable young women of your stories on the way! Come, Magda.'

'You wouldn't abandon me, alone and friendless, in a

foreign city?' he demanded, addressing himself to tender-hearted Magda. 'I might get lost.'

'We must take him with us,' whispered Magda. 'We can't go home without him. It would look so odd.'

'Ask the way!' Stefanie told him curtly, unimpressed by his supplication.

'I don't speak German.'

'You will find a way to make yourself understood, I am sure!'

She set off, determined to ignore him, which was difficult, as he strode briskly alongside her, taking one step to her every two. She felt herself walking faster and faster in a vain effort to lose him, so that their progress resembled an unequal race.

'Must we walk so fast?' he enquired, observing his companion becoming increasingly hot and breathless. 'I am a cavalryman, remember, and find all this marching hard on the feet.'

'Yes, must we?' complained Magda. 'He is going to come with us anyway, Stefanie, and I am getting a stitch in my side.'

'Oh, very well!' cried Stefanie, slowing down. 'Captain, I can only ask you to behave yourself.'

'Indeed, my dear, I shall make no such promise to *you*,' was the carefree reply.

When they arrived home, a familiar carriage stood waiting before the house.

'Hofrat von Letzberg,' whispered Magda. 'Do you think he might have news of Andreas?'

Their small party encountered von Letzberg on the stairs, drawing on his gloves and making his departure. The two men stared frostily at each other and exchanged curt nods.

'Excuse me, ladies, I beg you,' Léon said, leaving them to talk to the court councillor alone.

'I have just been discussing that young man with your Mama, my dears,' von Letzberg said. 'Let us move out into the street. I know it is cold, but I have a horror of being overheard.'

At any other time, this remark would have made Stefanie smile, for Hofrat von Letzberg, in his official capacity, received daily on his desk the reports of a whole network of spies. Perhaps it was the knowledge of that which made him so cautious now.

'As I was saying,' he continued in the relative security of the street. 'I am exceedingly sorry that you are obliged to suffer that gentleman's company. But, as I have explained to your dear mother, we cannot request his removal of the French, unless we lay some specific charge of misconduct against him. You—ah—have no complaint to make of him, my dear young ladies, mmn?' He fixed them with his cold, pale blue and slightly prominent eyes.

'No, sir,' they chorused together, a shade too quickly, and then exchanged guilty glances.

'None, sir,' Stefanie repeated firmly.

'He's been very nice, not at all alarming,' supplied Magda earnestly.

'Good . . . good. Well, I am pleased to hear it, of course. I will not keep you in the chill air any longer.'

'Sir,' Magda asked nervously, 'you have not had news of your nephew?'

'Ah . . .' von Letzberg brushed an invisible speck of dust from his sleeve. 'I have had no letter, if that is what you mean.'

'You don't even know where he is?' All of Magda's dejection echoed in her voice.

'Lieutenant von Letzberg is at Olmütz, with the Imperial family,' Andreas' uncle said. 'There, and in any future engagement with the enemy, I am confident he will do his duty.'

He climbed into his carriage and a footman closed the door. Before giving a signal to drive on, however, von Letzberg put his head out of the window and added,

'Regarding de Vaudry. The arch-fiend, Bonaparte, is already preparing to leave Vienna and take his confounded Imperial Guard with him. This will leave a force of occupation in the city, but, if events go as I foresee, not for long. You may soon be rid of your unwelcome guest.'

'Yes, sir,' Stefanie said quietly.

'I hate that man,' Magda said bitterly, as the carriage rolled away over the cobblestones. 'I wish he were not a friend of Mama's.'

'Magda!' Stephanie was astonished. 'I have never heard you say you hated anyone! I don't believe you could hate anyone, my poor sweet. Certainly not Andreas' uncle.'

'But that is just it! You see how he speaks of Andreas? So coldly, so distantly. He cares nothing for Andreas, nothing at all.'

'That cannot be so. He has left his considerable estates in Styria to Andreas in his will.'

'He has not done it for love, I'm certain. It is the promise of those wretched Styrian estates which keeps poor Andreas dancing attendance on that man whenever he is in Vienna. I should not be surprised if von Letzberg hopes Andreas will be killed, and then he can leave his wonderful lands to someone else!'

That chance meeting with Hofrat von Letzberg had given Stefanie a great deal to think over. As they retired to bed that night, she tapped on her mother's door.

'May I come in, Mama? I should like to talk about something with you.'

'Of course, my dear. That will be all, Mitzi.'

Stefanie sat down and waited until the maid had left. Her mother was seated before her dressing mirror, her long thick hair hanging onto her shoulders, and wearing a loose negligée. She was indeed a remarkably handsome woman, Stefanie thought, and wondered, not for the first time, why the seemingly unemotional Hofrat von Letzberg, of all men, should be the one . . .

'Mama,' she ventured, 'I really don't know how to put this, but what do you think will happen to us all?'

'Happen? In what way, child?'

'That's what I can't explain. Mama, I have such a, such a bad feeling about the future. As if something dreadful was going to happen, to Austria and to us.'

'Is that because the French are here in Vienna, perhaps?' the Baroness asked, toying with a silver-backed hairbrush.

'That is what I tell myself. Certainly, Captain de Vaudry is confident that the French will always beat anyone else! But, even before they came, I had this odd feeling, a sort of premonition. I can't speak of it no Magda. She would be so upset.'

'I wish she had not lost her heart so young,' the Baroness sighed. 'Now she must bear the misery of separation. But, Stefanie, you must not be afraid.' The Baroness lowered her voice. 'Ignaz von Letzberg was here whilst you were out and we had a long discussion. As you know, Hofrat von Letzberg is in a position to be informed of the progress of war, and he tells me—' The Baroness paused. 'I tell you this in *strictest* confidence, my dear. Not a word of our conversation must reach the ear of our guest. Ignaz tells me that considerable rein-forcements are on the way from Russia and, even now, are joining forces with Prince Kutuzov's army some-where in Moravia. Together with our Austrians they will make an immense and unbeatable army! When Bona-parte learns of it, he will be forced to retreat, to sue for peace. He could not risk his own troops against so formidable a foe. It would be a slaughter. He is outnum-bered, his army is dispersed, he has no supply lines. His men live off the countryside and now, in winter, the countryside is bare. Bonaparte will have neither meat for his men nor fodder for his horses. Do you not see?

All will be well for Austria!' The Baroness gripped her daughter's hand. 'Believe me!'

Stefanie looked down at her mother's white hand which held hers so tightly that the knuckles stood out sharply. 'This is wonderful news, Mama, and I'm so glad to hear you say it,' she said a little soberly. 'But Magda fears so for Andreas, what am I to say to her? She asked Hofrat von Letzberg if he had news, but he had none of his nephew. Mama, do you think he really cares about Andreas? Magda says not, because he is always so . . . cold . . .' Stefanie faltered.

'Oh!' The Baroness threw up her hands. 'You young people! You think everyone must wear his heart upon his sleeve as you do. If he does not, then he can have no heart. Magda thinks no one can love Andreas as she does. She is wrong.' She leaned towards Stefanie again and put her beringed fingers on her daughter's arm. 'Tell Magda, I *know* that Hofrat von Letzberg is quite devoted to his nephew. In fact, if anything were to happen to that boy, I do not think Ignaz would ever recover—' the Baroness broke off. 'But we must not think of these things. Tell Magda not to worry, and don't worry yourself. Goodnight, child.'

'Goodnight, Mama,' Stefanie kissed her mother's forehead and left.

'Daughters, daughters,' sighed the Baroness to herself, picking up the hairbrush. 'When they were little, I had such plans for brilliant matches for them both. And now what? One is hardly out of the cradle, but she is in love with a boy little older than herself, and the other is in danger of falling in love, despite herself, with an attractive daredevil of a Frenchman who will very likely break her heart. Yet, I thank God at this time that I have no sons—for both Andreas and the Captain may be cold in their graves by Christmas, and what will mean an Austrian victory to my daughters, if they are left to mourn and light candles? What a thing is war.'

CHAPTER
FIVE

For the next two days the Captain's behaviour was impeccable. Even Hofrat von Letzberg could have found no fault. He played cards with them, teaching them *vingt-et-un*. He read aloud to them from a battered edition of Racine's plays discovered in a cupboard, ~~~ing the speeches with such verve and energy that ~~~ Baroness declared he should have been an actor. ~~~ he engaged Stefanie to teach him to waltz, accompanied—with frequent wrong notes—by Magda at the piano.

Stefanie was at first very nervous at the thought of being once again in his arms, but as these lessons were conducted most decorously under the watchful eye of the Baroness, they proceeded with nothing more untoward than a great deal of harmless merriment.

'Monsieur de Vaudry, you must not look so ferocious!' exclaimed the Baroness.

'I am concentrating, madame. I fear to tread upon my teacher's pettitcoats.'

'Then you must learn to concentrate with a smile! My dear man, you will frighten your partners into fits.'

'Alas, madame, it seems I do that already.' He exchanged a glance with Stefanie.

She flushed and fixed her eyes on his white waistcoat. 'You are all wrong, Captain,' she told him crossly. 'One—two—no, no!'

'It is not my fault. It is the fault of the musician. Mademoiselle Magda, you play out of time.'

'Indeed, monsieur, I do not!' objected Magda. 'I know

I get some of the notes wrong, but not the timing. I am most particular. It is you, you have no sense of the rhythm of the piece at all.'

'And is that the same young lady speaking now, who confessed to being so afraid of me when I first came to this house?'

'We did not know you then,' said Magda, turning back the pages of her music and striking an opening chord comprising so many wrong notes all together that the Baroness clapped her hands to her ears and cried:

'Enough, enough! Captain, please be seated. I am sure you need a rest. You may continue to read to us from *Britannicus*, where you left off yesterday. Maria-Magdalena, how often have I told you, you do not practise enough?'

Magda closed the lid of the piano with some relief and the Captain released Stefanie, but not before he had caught her gaze and twitched a quizzical eyebrow at her. Stefanie sat down, spending longer than necessary to smooth out her skirts, and they prepared to listen to the play.

But hardly had the Captain started, than there came the sound of a sudden distant explosion. It was quickly followed by another, which made the windows rattle. The Frenchman put down the book and, with a murmured excuse, went to the windows. Opening them, he leaned out, listening intently. Inside the room, it would have been possible to hear a pin drop.

Boom! The crystal drops of the chandelier swayed and tinkled like Chinese bells. The Captain grunted and closed the windows.

'What is it, monsieur?' the Baroness asked.

'Cannon, madame.' He paused. 'Russian cannon.'

'The Russians have come back?' Magda cried loudly.

'No, mademoiselle, it will be their rear guard, in an engagement with our forces.'

'So near . . .' Stefanie murmured.

'And yet so far . . . I do not think, mademoiselle, that Kutuzov is about to retake Vienna, so I must warn you against building your hopes too high!'

She gave him an angry look. 'You are very sure, Captain.'

'Listen!' he told her, raising a hand. The distant cannon roared again. 'That, *chère mademoiselle*, is the voice from a bronze mouth cast according to Gribeauval —French cannon. Neither the Austrians nor the Russians have yet gained the mastery over our artillery.'

'Such confidence, Captain! The French are, then, invincible?'

He gave her a dry smile. 'In War, as in Love, mademoiselle!' He picked up the book and calmly began again to read from where he had stopped at the interruption.

The cannon continued to sound throughout the afternoon, but towards evening fell silent. The captain seemed unaffected by it, although once or twice Stefanie saw him frown slightly, as if he calculated the distance away of the engagement. But by common consent, no one referred to the cannonade, even though the window panes continued to shiver and the ornaments to sing out in reply.

The following morning, Sunday, was dry and sunny, if cold. It was to prove a day Stefanie would never forget, even though many more eventful days were to follow. But already it had seemed to her that the cannonade of the previous afternoon had been a signal, heralding events which were to remain for ever etched in her memory.

It began, harmlessly enough, with the Baroness and her daughters preparing to go to morning Mass at the Schottenkirche—that one of Vienna's churches founded centuries before by Irish, not Scots, monks.

'What about the Captain?' asked Magda. 'Would he want to come?'

'I doubt it,' said Stefanie, setting her hat on her blonde

curls with a firm hand, and tying the strings.

'We can ask him, I suppose,' the Baroness said doubt-fully. 'Someone must have taught him some religion at some time in his life. But I have not seen him this morning. Joachim, is the Captain awake yet?'

Joachim snorted. 'Awake? Sleeping like a dead man, and I'm not surprised at it. After you all went to bed last night, *he* went out. Didn't come back till nearly three in the morning, and then he was tipped out of a *Fiaker* onto the street outside this door, much the worse for brandy. I wonder you didn't hear the noise. It's a blessing you didn't, dear ladies. He got himself into a tangle with his sword and the step of the *Fiaker* and fell out onto the cobbles, cursing in every language known to man! I had to go down in my nightshirt and bring him in. I gave him a piece of my mind, too. And to that fool of a *Fiaker* driver who stood there laughing.

'Goodness,' said Magda in awe. 'I hope he didn't hurt himself. I wonder where he had been.'

'Oh, I can tell you where he'd been!' growled Joachim. 'And with whom—or with what! He gave me his jacket to brush off the mud from the cobblestones. There wasn't only mud on it, there was a lot of long female hair, too, and such a smell of cheap perfume—'

'Thank you, Joachim, that will be enough!' inter-rupted the Baroness sharply.

Stefanie turned away so that no one could see her mortification. So that was the result of her laborious attempts to teach him to waltz! He slipped out to perfect his new accomplishment with the amenable damsels to be found in Vienna's less respectable cabarets. Nor, no doubt, was that all.

'Why, I am jealous!' she thought suddenly in wonder and resentment. But then she thought: 'What should I expect? No doubt he wants some other entertainment than what he may find here, reading aloud to us!'

The knowledge hurt, all the same, because she knew

he awaited only the slightest sign of encouragement from her. He had received that encouragement once, and she read a question in his eyes each time he looked at her, though he said nothing. Was it surprising that what he might not receive here, he had sought elsewhere?

'I think that answers your question, Magda,' said her mother. 'I do not think we need expect our guest's company.'

As might have been expected, the city was alive with rumour, following Saturday's sound of cannon which no one had been able to ignore.

'I tell you, the French are retreating,' a sturdy fellow in a green huntsman's jacket and leather breeches, was insisting, to a knot of his fellow citizens in their Sunday best. 'Anyone could tell that the Russian artillery was getting the better of it. They sent the French running, you'll see.'

His confidence seemed to Stefanie to equal the captain's and she began to wonder whether, in fact, the fortunes of the French army might not have changed, and, as they drove homewards, they came upon what appeared to be grim confirmation of this suggestion.

As the carriage was about to turn from the Graben into the Kärtnerstrasse, it caught up with a flat, open, sideless cart, lumbering along. Magda, glancing out of the window, gave a sudden shriek.

'What is it?' Stefanie asked in alarm.

Magda pointed silently to two long, stiff shapes, roughly covered by a sodden cloth, stretched on the cart.

'Dead men!' she whispered in a strangled voice.

'Impossible, they can't be . . .' Stefanie began.

The open cart gave a lurch over the rough cobbles and an arm fell loosely from under the cloth, and hung limply over the edge. White, lifeless fingers brushed against the rim of the cartwheel. The arm was clad in blue French infantry uniform, and a steady stream of water dripped from the sleeve.

The Baroness leaned forward quickly and dragged down the blind, shutting out the grisly sight.

'Sit up straight, Maria-Magdalena,' she ordered. 'Stefanie, you are slouching, too.'

'Yes, Mama,' they said dutifully, and after that no one spoke until they were home.

'Is the Captain out of bed yet?' the Baroness demanded of Joachim, when they were indoors.

'Yes, *gnädige Frau*, and gone out. After you left, someone brought a message for him. Whatever it was, it woke him up well enough! He yelled for hot water, and when I took it in, there he was, hopping about on one foot, struggling into his breeches, and in as foul a temper as you could wish to see. He rushed out of the house, half-shaved and pulling on his coat. I don't know where he went, *gnädige Frau*, but he wanted to know the direction of the river.'

'The river?' cried Stefanie.

'Ah, Fräulein,' Joachim said regretfully, shaking his head. 'It's too much to hope that he went off to put an end to his wretched existence!'

'One would hope not! But he gave no hint at all?'

'No, and I didn't ask him,' snapped Joachim testily. 'I don't know and I don't want to know what the French cur is up to. Perhaps he went fishing, for all I care!' He stomped off.

All these events had upset Magda badly. She went to lie down on her bed with a cologne soaked handkerchief on her brow, and when Stefanie looked in later, she saw her sister had fallen asleep.

'We promised Liesl we would go and see her this afternoon, Mama,' she told her mother. 'But Magda is sleeping and I don't want to wake her. Will it be all right if I go alone?'

Liesl was an old servant, living in a tiny apartment in one of the numerous tenements of the city, on a small pension.

'I suppose so, my dear, but take care. Don't stay late.'

Stefanie set off on foot. The visit to Liesl was a regular feature whilst the family was in Vienna, and took place about once a month. The old woman had no family, and lived alone. Surrounded by noisy neighbours busy about their own business, she depended on visits by the sisters. They always walked there, for on Sunday afternoons Wenzel, the coachman, had his free time. In the summer, Stefanie knew, Wenzel spent this free time at the Prater with various lady friends. But in the winter, he spent it in taverns, until the family was ready for their regular annual journey to the Moravian estate, on which he would drive them. Wenzel was a Czech, and for him the annual journey was a journey home to his village.

The Baroness was a considerate employer and served with devotion by all her servants. Nearly all servants in Vienna informed upon their employers to the police—it was one of the peculiarities of Viennese life which amazed and shocked foreigners, but which the Viennese accepted with equanimity and even humour. Stefanie often wondered if their own servants did so, although Wenzel had once told her, in a hoarse and surreptitious whisper, that 'no one from your gracious lady mother's household goes running to others with tittle-tattle!'

Stefanie hoped this was true, and was inclined to believe it was—which must make their household almost unique amongst Vienna's wealthier ones. On the other hand, Hofrat von Letzberg's peculiar position as favoured and intimate visitor probably rendered servants' reports unnecessary. Unless, of course, they reported on Hofrat von Letzberg to others, a thought which gave Stefanie a certain malicious pleasure.

Absorbed in this and other conjectures as she walked along, she had failed to notice that she was walking straight towards two pig-tailed French Grenadiers whose jovial, if slightly unsteady, progress indicated that they had recently left a tavern. She was brought to realise the situation when an arm encircled her waist with rough familiarity and a voice, redolent of wine, declared: 'What, *ma belle*, all alone?'

'Let me go!' she cried indignantly, struggling to free herself.

'Well, the pretty little lady speaks French! Where did you learn to do that, eh, my beauty?'

'You are indiscreet, Jeannot,' admonished his companion with drunken dignity. 'French is the language of pillow-talk, isn't that so, mam'zelle, *hein*?' He hiccupped.

'How dare you? Let go of me at once!' Stefanie managed to free herself with an effort, thanks to her new admirer being uncertain on his feet.

'That's it,' cried a raucous voice. 'Insult our Viennese women! You'll soon be running for home, you French scum!'

Startled, she looked up and saw that a group of pallid faced young men, journeymen tailors by the look of them, had gathered a short distance away.

'Didn't you hear the Russian guns?' jeered another, and the first, stooping quickly, scooped up a handful of mud from the street and flung it at the nearer of the two Grenadiers, spattering his uniform.

With lurid oaths, the two infantrymen lurched forward and, even given their state of inebriation and numerical inferiority, might well have made short work of their tormentors. But at that moment a shout of warning and the sound of running feet heralded two French officers who appeared round the corner of the street.

Stefanie took advantage of the diversion to dart into a nearby doorway where she cowered back into the dark recess. She could hear a great deal of shouting in French and German, and the clatter of feet on the cobbles. Then there was silence, and a tall shadow fell across her hiding place.

'And just what do you think you are doing, wandering around the streets alone, on today of all days?' Léon demanded.

He was slightly breathless and his hair fell untidily over his forehead. He held his hat in his hand, and there was a smear of blood above one eyebrow from a small cut.

'Oh, it's you,' Stefanie exclaimed. 'I didn't realise . . . What are you doing here?'

'I asked first. What are *you* doing here?'

'Going to see Liesl—an old servant of ours. She lives near here.'

'I'll walk with you there,' he said, putting on his hat. 'But you are very stupid to come out alone today.'

'I did not expect to see people throwing stones and mud, or I should not have done! But there has been nothing like it since the French came, so why should I expect it today?'

'Why? Because your compatriots of the street just now, in company with the rest of Vienna, heard the guns yesterday, and have suddenly acquired reserves of courage noticeably lacking before.'

'Everyone is saying the French are retreating,' she ventured.

'They are wrong, as both they and you will be disappointed to hear.' After a pause he went on in a stony voice, 'I have been down to the river. The watermen of the Danube have a new employment today. They are engaged in bringing to shore the bodies of our soldiers which have been brought downstream from yesterday's engagement. This indicates, of course, that we suffered some losses, and no doubt gave rise to the rumours.'

'I know about your dead,' Stefanie said quietly. 'We passed a cart . . .'

He glanced at her. 'If you'd taken a closer look you'd have seen no wounds on them.'

She was puzzled. 'What do you mean?'

'I mean, mademoiselle, that the Russians would seem to have taken to drowning their French prisoners.'

'They would not do anything so barbaric!' She was horrified.

'Why not? It's a change from their usual practice of cutting off the ears of captured French.' He pulled out his handkerchief and wiped his forehead of the blood which had begun to trickle down the side of his crooked nose.

'You are hurt,' she said in some concern. 'How did it happen?'

'It is nothing. One of your bold Viennese compatriots threw a well-aimed stone at me—from behind a convenient wall, of course! Tomorrow, when he finds the French are not retreating after all, he will lose his new-found courage in a flash, and be as meek as you please.'

'Liesl lives here,' Stefanie said abruptly, stopping before a tall, narrow old building. So he thought the Viennese cowards for surrendering their city so easily! Probably he despised all civilians, even her and Magda and their mother. She turned to face him beneath the doorway. Above her head the house front was painted with an ancient and weatherworn representation of St Hubert's miraculous meeting with the Stag.

'I will wait for you here,' Léon said, 'in the company of the huntsmen's patron, and escort you to your home.'

His tone seemed to underline that he thought she had behaved foolishly, but she knew that his offer was not only courteous, but wise, and to refuse it in the circumstances would indeed be foolishness. She nodded her agreement.

Stefanie began to climb the steep, narrow staircase, but at the *mezzanin* she paused and looked back, her hand resting on a wooden rail polished smooth by hundreds of palms. In the doorway below, Léon's tall, long-legged figure was silhouetted darkly against the daylight from the street. As she watched, he tipped his hat forward slightly over his eyes, and leaned back against the doorpost, folding his arms, prepared to wait for her. For all his nonchalant stance, he seemed all too obvious there, a French officer, alone. There was something else too, something to which she could not put a name, but which caused a strange physical stirring within her at the sight of him.

Stefanie bit her lip and picked up her skirts to run back lightly down the staircase.

'Ready so soon?' he asked, affecting surprise.

'No, no . . .' She took his sleeve and pulled his arm, anxious for him to be out of the danger of the open street. Speaking quickly, she said, 'You had better come up with me. With things as they are, to stand about alone in the street might invite some sort of attack.'

'Afraid for me, are you?' he asked, with his crooked and disreputable grin.

'Oh, I am sure you can look after yourself!' she told him promptly. 'But I don't want to have to run to the window every five minutes to make sure you are all right.'

They climbed the narrow dark staircase, scented at every turn with the smells of crowded humanity, soap-suds and pickled cabbage, tobacco smoke and fried onion, all mingled in a kind of fog.

'This is no place for you,' he observed disapprovingly. 'Though I suppose you must do your duty by the poor. *La noblesse oblige . . .*'

'*I* don't mind the smell!' she defended herself.

'Well, then, it is no place for *me*,' he grumbled, taking off his hat and waving it before his nose.

'Then wait in the street, after all. Don't blame me if someone throws half a brick at you.'

'What? And refuse an invitation to follow a pretty girl

up a staircase?' he returned, grinning impudently at her. 'Lead on, *ma belle*, I have the highest hopes!'

'You will be disappointed, Captain.'

Old Liesl greeted them with pleasure and did not seem particularly surprised to see a French officer in her tiny, but beautifully kept, sitting room.

'I have brought you coffee, Liesl,' Stefanie said, producing a small package.

'Coffee, my pretty one? Then we shall have good coffee with our strudel. I have made apple strudel especially for you, my dove.'

'Liesl makes the best strudel in all Vienna,' Stefanie said to Léon.

'Only sit down there, and tell the gentleman to mind his head on the hanging lamp. Does the poor man speak no German? Well, he must learn! How is your gracious lady mother? Thank her for the coffee. To be sure, no one can afford to buy it in this house . . .' Liesl prattled on from the curtained recess which constituted her kitchen. 'It's all the fault of the paper money. Worthless stuff, not like a good coin. But "they" have taken all the silver and nearly all the copper for this war. They take our good money, and give us bits of paper—*bancozettel* —just as "they" take our children, and give us back cripples. It is always the children of the poor who must go! Every young working man who cannot show his employment is necessary here in Vienna has had to go to the army, did you know? My neighbour's son has been taken, only seventeen . . .'

Stefanie did not deem it prudent to translate any of this to Léon, who, barred from the conversation, had gone to look out of the window. Now he said: 'There's a gipsy down in the street, stopping people to tell their fortunes. Have someone bring her up. She can tell mine—and yours.'

'A gipsy?' Stefanie said doubtfully. 'I would rather not. They frighten me. They see things we do not.'

'Pah! It's only an amusement. They make it all up out of their heads.'

Liesl, informed of this intention, asked shrewdly, 'Has the gentleman any good coin, some groschen or a kreuzer? For the gipsy won't take paper money.'

'The gipsy has good sense,' Léon said, digging in his pocket. 'I have this.' He held up a *huszás*, the Hungarian equivalent of the Austrian *zwanziger* or twenty kreuzer piece. 'I won it at cards.'

'You will give all that to a gipsy?' cried Liesl. 'For that she will promise you the world!'

'I am a Dragoon in the service of the Emperor,' he said. 'The world is already mine. Fetch up the gipsy woman.'

Stefanie did not like the idea but had to acquiesce. Her doubts were given new force by the sight of the gipsy. She was a woman of perhaps thirty or thirty-five, sturdily built but poorly dressed. Her flat face, never attractive, was further disfigured by the ravages of small-pox, and her eyes were like those of a wild animal, darting about the little room, seeing all but betraying nothing. It seemed to Stefanie the eyes looked at and through her, and all round her, at the same time. Around her head the gipsy wore a tightly bound rag, but on her dirty fingers were curiously wrought gold rings of some value.

'Ladies first,' Léon said. 'Give her your hand.'

There was nothing Stefanie wanted to do less. It was all she could do not to recoil physically at the touch of the gipsy's fingers as they took hers.

'The pretty lady has a good hand, a lucky hand,' crooned the woman. Her dark eyes flickered from Léon to Stefanie and back again. 'You will make a fine marriage.'

'What does she say?' Léon asked.

'Oh, the usual nonsense,' Stefanie tried to pull her hand away, but the gipsy held it fast.

'Do you not want to know the man you will marry, pretty lady? I see him clearly. He is a fine, handsome man, a soldier, perhaps. Together you and he will make many fine children—'

Stefanie pulled her hand free sharply and snapped. 'You talk nonsense!'

'Let her read my palm,' Léon said, chuckling, and Stefanie gave him a suspicious look. She began to wonder if, indeed, his German was as poor as he claimed it was, or whether he understood more than he cared to admit. He held out his hand towards the gipsy, palm uppermost. Stefanie noticed for the first time that he had long, delicate tapering fingers and a slim, elegant palm. An aristocrat's hand, she thought. Neither Revolution, nor Terror, Napoleon or the Dragoons could alter the legacy of ancestry.

The gipsy leaned forward to take his fingers, but suddenly recoiled, drawing back her own hand sharply. For a second, something akin to fear showed in the wild eyes. 'There is death in this hand,' she muttered. 'I will not touch it!'

Stefanie felt as though a cold breeze blew over her, and she shivered, although it was hot and stuffy in the little room. Unwillingly, she translated to Léon what the gipsy had said.

'Let her read my fortune anyway,' he said easily. 'I have long lived with death. I set little store by her predictions. But I want something for my money.'

The gipsy bent over his palm, taking care not to touch it.

'I see many men, many men marching. They come from the East, and the Archangel will lead them.'

'I don't understand it,' Stefanie said, translating. 'It makes no sense.'

'I do!' he said sharply. ' "The Archangel" is what the Russians call Czar Alexander. Ask her, where and when she saw these men.'

'But she saw them in your hand.'

'Rubbish! She saw them with her own eyes, or others of her people have, and the word has passed among them.'

But the gipsy was unforthcoming, maintaining obstinately that she read it in the palm.

'They do not like outsiders to know their movements, I fancy,' Stefanie said. 'But news travels rapidly amongst them.'

'Then tell her I would know more about these Russian reinforcements she sees "in my hand".'

The gipsy was sullen now and seemed anxious to get away. 'I see many men, many with the mark of death on them. I see blood, a great battle!' She hunted in her pocket and took out the *huszás* he had given her, flinging the coin down onto the table where it rolled in a circle, glinting mockingly. 'And I will not take his money. It brings bad luck!'

'Here,' Stefanie said, also wanting the woman to leave, 'I have a little money. Take this . . .' She held out a handful of small change.

As the gipsy stretched out her hand to take the groschen, Léon, with a lightning movement, seized her wrist, and although the gipsy twisted and turned furiously, cursing him, he held her fast.

'She must finish her predictions first! Or I will take her before General Clarke, the commandant of the city.'

'Very well!' the gipsy spat at him. 'But tell the Frenchman to take his hand from me. His touch brings ill fortune.'

'Right!' Léon said grimly, releasing her. 'This battle, when will it be fought?'

'Soon, soon, before the next snow comes . . .' The gipsy began to rock slightly from side to side, cradling her arms as if they held an invisible child. The action was full of an indescribable menace. Her voice crooned in a sing-song way, and her eyes glazed as if she were in a trance. 'The place is ready. I see it. Now it is quiet and at peace. Soon it will be filled by the voices of the guns and soaked by the blood of the dying.'

'And it has a name, this place?' he asked sarcastically.

The gipsy shot him a malevolent look in which hatred was mixed with triumph.

'It is called Austerlitz!' she hissed.

CHAPTER
SIX

'WHY do you let it upset you?' Léon asked as they walked home. 'The gods of war might know where a battle is to be fought, but no human can, not even a gipsy. She plucked the name out of the air. She was afraid I would take her to General Clarke.'

'Even if she did, why that name? Of all the places to choose, why Austerlitz? I told you, it is a little town, not so very far from our country place. It is quiet and peaceful and sleepy, and no one ever goes there. Why choose it?'

'She did not know you, I suppose?' he asked thoughtfully, picking up her hand and tucking her arm through his. 'Gipsies are quick to weave any little knowledge they have of you into their fortune-telling.'

She felt confused and frightened and was glad of his arm. 'No, no, she didn't know me. She couldn't. I've never seen her before.'

'She might have seen *you*. Her people are wanderers. You've told me how the gipsies pass through the Moravian villages. She might have seen you.'

'I suppose so . . .' Stefanie was unconvinced. 'But it's horrible, horrible—a dreadful omen!'

'Now, what should I do,' he asked, 'if I were as superstitious as you? I'm sorry I had the gipsy read our palms. I thought it would be amusing. If I were to believe such nonsense, why, I'd be in a poor state! And I would have credited you with more common-sense. It was unfortunate that the gipsy named a place so close to your Moravian estates, but it is not an omen. Trust me. Come

79

now, you are not a little chambermaid, walking with her beau in the Prater, and all agog to hear the gipsy's warning!'

'I dare say you are right,' she said unhappily. 'Perhaps she has seen me before. Perhaps it's not impossible.'

'That's the spirit!' After a while, he added in a casual tone, 'Tell me about that part of the country. What's it like?'

'It is as I told you, quiet, peaceful, rolling countryside. Here and there a country estate such as ours, and dotted with little villages of just one street. The women stand in the doorways of their wooden cottages and gossip, and the babies cry and the dogs bark, and the only excitement is when a pig gets into someone's vegetable patch! At Austerlitz itself there is a small *Schloss* belonging to the Kaunitz family—that's a very famous noble house, but it is the only place of note for miles around.'

'No highroad?'

'No. The nearest is the highroad from Brünn to Olmütz, but you must leave that and turn onto country roads which are little more than tracks, and at this time of year are so muddy they are sometimes scarcely passable.'

'No obstacles, then, to putting a few hundred cavalry charging across? No rivers?'

'No large ones, just streams. There are the marshes, of course. In winter they flood and freeze so that they are quite iced over. The country people call them the lakes, but they are hardly true lakes.' She pulled her arm from his with a jerk and turned to face him. 'Why are you asking all this? You *do* believe the gipsy, you do!'

'I most certainly do not!' he returned firmly. 'But I'm naturally curious to hear about any new piece of country, especially if there is the remotest chance that one day I shall be thundering across it with a hundred others, brandishing a sabre and half-blinded by the mud flung up by the fellow in front. I want to know if I'm likely to gallop straight into a ditch!' He grinned at her.

'Why, you *enjoy* it!' Stefanie exclaimed incredulously, struck by something in his tone. 'You love it. Despite all you said to me about being afraid, and people being killed, you love the action, and the noise, perhaps the thrill of it all.'

'I know no other life, and there is no life, nothing on this earth, like it. The waiting is the worst . . .' His eyes stared into the distance seeing, not the buildings about them, but the ranks of mounted men. 'The horses are nervous. They hear the thunder of the guns, and know they will be ridden towards it. They start to prance about, even the most seasoned old campaigner of them, and you must talk to them to soothe them. That's not so easy when your own stomach is tied into knots and your heart seems as though it will burst out of your chest and every breath is painful. Then the signal is given, the horses prick their ears and the whole squadron starts forward at a trot, moving as one being, and you are part of it. All the knots in your stomach unravel and the blood starts to race in your veins. You are totally committed and cannot turn back, nor do you want to. Even when you are galloping down on the great guns and see them spewing red death at you, you have no thought of retreating, only to get down there and sabre the gunners, poor devils, and silence the great monsters which cut wide swathes through the squares like a sickle through corn. A cavalry charge is a thing of hot blood and passion. It is like love. It burns a man's very soul.'

'Be silent!' she cried at him. 'I don't want to know about it. It's all horrible and barbaric! Nor shall I tell you another thing about Austerlitz or the district about it. I betray my country in talking to you of it. I shall tell you nothing, nothing more! You may ask away as much as you wish.' She was angry and frightened.

'What? Think I'm a spy, do you? A sinister secret agent, wheedling information out of you? I leave all that kind of thing to more subtle minds than mine.' He reached out to take her shoulders and shake her gently. 'Listen, from all you've said, Austerlitz sounds an unlikely place for Kutuzov to decide to make his stand.'

'Indeed, Captain?' she said icily. 'Kindly release me.'

'Still mistrust me?' He let his hands drop back by his sides. 'I'm not one of those devious fellows like your Mama's admirer, old von Letzberg.'

'Hofrat von Letzberg is not my mother's admirer!' She informed him coldly. 'He is an old and trusted friend and adviser to my family.'

'Ho, ho! Even you cannot be so naive as to believe he is no more than that! Besides, to suggest *that* is all he is, would be to insult your mama, who is a most attractive and admirable woman. What's more, she has reached that best of ages, when a woman has acquired experience, and learned discretion, eh?' He chuckled and, reaching out, pinched Stefanie's cheek gently in a familiar manner.

She struck his hand aside furiously. 'How dare you? How dare you speak of my mother with such disrespect?'

'I don't. I have the greatest respect and regard for her. In fact, had your mother not such a beautiful and desirable elder daughter, I might be tempted to try and displace von Letzberg. That would be amusing, I think.'

'You are unspeakable!' she said, aghast. 'All they say of the French is true. Neither age, nor a woman's standing in society, prevent you entertaining the . . . the basest designs!'

'Nonsense. How seriously you take everything. I have said nothing to you I have not said to your mama, and she by no means reacted so violently.'

'I don't believe you, you would not dare!' she raged, stamping her foot on the cobblestones.

He did not reply but strolled along, unconcerned.

After a while, she asked in a more subdued voice in

which the curiosity could not be suppressed. 'What did she reply?'

He burst into laughter. 'But now, *ma petite*,' he said, shaking a finger at her infuriatingly, 'you ask me to be indiscreet. I cannot be that. You will have to stay eaten up with curiosity—and it will be very good for you.'

'Hofrat von Letzberg must go to the French straight away and insist upon that man's removal from this house!' stormed Stefanie to her mother. 'His behaviour is inexcusable. He is nothing but a rake. He has no morals at all.'

'Goodness,' observed the Baroness. 'How very red in the face you are, Stefanie. Am I to understand that our guest has so far forgotten himself as to make, let us say, certain suggestions to you?'

'No, no, not me! He . . . he speaks most disrespectfully of you, and says it is out of admiration. He is a complete scoundrel, I tell you.'

'Oh, I don't think so,' remarked the Baroness, snipping off a length of embroidery thread with perfect calm. 'I don't doubt that his morals are a little free, but that is to be expected, and is far from being the same as having no morals at all. He is a military man, young, good-looking . . . if he had not had his share of amorous adventures, it would be very odd, and the world must have changed very much since I was young.'

'Then it is true, as he says, that he has paid you all manner of compliments?'

The Baroness gave a little laugh. 'Indeed, I did have a most delightful and entertaining conversation with Monsieur de Vaudry yesterday. Your captain is very charming—and very bold.'

'He is not *my* captain!' returned Stefanie forcefully. 'I trust, Mama, you put him in his place? Told him you would report the matter to the city commandant, made it clear you would not allow such familiarity?'

'Oh, yes, yes. That is what he *expected* me to say! Really, Stefanie, what *can* you imagine? It was an amusement on his part, a *divertissement*. I told him he was very impudent,' the Baroness touched her hair and glanced into a nearby mirror, 'and that I quite wished I was twenty years younger.'

'Mama!' cried Stefanie, in disbelief.

'And, do you know?' concluded the Baroness serenely. 'I do believe, that just for a moment, when I said *that*, our gallant Dragoon looked quite confused.'

There was a silence and then Stefanie collapsed onto the nearest chair with a peal of laughter. 'Oh, Mama, you are magnificent! How I wish I'd seen it.'

'Oh, you know,' the Baroness smoothed out her embroidery, 'at forty-four, to receive the compliments of a handsome and virile man of seven and twenty, can hardly be disagreeable—even if we both knew he did not mean it! He is an attractive rascal, our captain, but bred a gentleman. Have a care, Stefanie, I dare say he collects hearts, and it would be a pity to make him a present of yours. Now, tell me, how do you think my embroidery progresses?'

Despite her best efforts, Stefanie could not put the gipsy's prediction out of her head. She did not mean to confide her fears to Magda, but it was difficult to hide them from someone to whom she was so close. She confessed it all eventually one night as they were going to bed, sitting hunched on the pillows in her nightgown, with her arms wrapped about her knees.

Magda, perched on the end of the bed, listened wide-eyed.

'How horrid, Stefanie. I should have fainted away, when she said that, I know I should. Did the Captain believe it?'

'He says not. He says the gipsy "plucked the name out of the air".'

'I dare say she did.' Magda fell to twisting her curls around a finger as was her habit. 'She might have seen you before. Or why should she name Austerlitz?'

'Exactly!' Stefanie leaned forward. 'Such a tiny place. Why not Pressburg, or Troppau, or Olmütz—' she broke off. 'Oh, Magda, I'm sorry.'

'Andreas is at Olmütz,' Magda said in a flat voice. 'Or I think he is. Perhaps he's already been sent somewhere else.'

'I could bite my tongue out,' said Stefanie contritely. 'What the gipsy did to me in naming Austerlitz, I have done to you in naming Olmütz.'

'There's going to be a great battle, anyway,' Magda said with dismal resignation, 'and does it matter where? Andreas will be there, wherever it is. He said it would give him a chance to distinguish himself. I believe he was almost looking forward to it.'

'They are all the same,' Stefanie said grimly. 'You should hear the Captain talk of the excitement, and the blood pulsing in the veins and all that sort of thing. He likes it. He likes galloping about sabring the enemy and risking getting his own head sliced from his shoulders. It's just some sort of terrible game to him. He talks of fear, but in a strange way I even believe he relishes that. He is like Andreas, he knows there will be a battle and he is looking forward to it. Men are brutes, all of them, even the nicest, like Andreas.'

'And Monsieur de Vaudry? Is he a nice brute?' asked Magda with a little smile.

'How can he be nice? He says the most outrageous and despicable things, and takes pleasure in behaving badly.'

'He teases you, Stefanie,' said practical little Magda in her direct way. 'Why can't you see it? He says all those things to make you cross. He likes it when your eyes "flash sparks". He told me so.'

'*Did* he? The Captain, it seems, talks freely with everyone!' Stefanie slipped her feet under the feather quilt and lay back on the pillows. 'What else did he say, may I ask?'

'Oh . . . he thinks you very beautiful. He thinks you have the finest eyes of any woman he has ever seen. That's when he spoke about the sparks.' Magda blew out the candle and scrambled into bed. 'And he said, "your sister is afraid to trust her heart". I think he is a little in love with you. But isn't that what you wanted?'

'No, no! I don't want him to be in love with me at all! I know I *said* I did, but I was speaking stupidly then. He had made me angry, and I wanted to be revenged on him. He still makes me angry—but he makes me laugh as well. When I am with him, I feel so . . . so different. Before he came, life was so empty, and when he is gone, I don't know what I shall do. If I really think about it, it frightens me. You know, Magda, I often feel as though you were the elder of the two of us. You are so *sure*!' Stefanie stared into the dark. 'I am not in love with him, you understand!' she added belatedly, as an after-thought.

'I like him,' Magda said, snuggling down under the quilt. 'I just wish he wasn't French—then you *could* fall in love with him! Brrrh . . . it's cold. I don't fancy the journey to Moravia at all.'

With all that had happened, Stefanie had almost forgotten that they were due to depart for Moravia. But the Baroness had not, and the following day Mitzi came to tell the girls she would pack their linen that morning.

'But what about Captain de Vaudry?' Stefanie asked her mother.

'Indeed, it is very awkward,' the Baroness sighed. 'I do not like to leave him here with just the servants, though they will look after him very well. I had thought, he would be gone by now. Nearly all the French have gone. The Corsican himself stayed but two days! However, they will expect us in the country, and it is too late now to send a message saying we cannot come.

Monsieur de Vaudry will have to fend for himself, he will be used to that. At least, here he will be comfortable.'

The rest of the morning was spent packing, a tiring and frustrating business. There would not be room for much luggage and there was much arguing over what to take. Magda crammed in a mysterious package wrapped in a piece of old velvet curtain. It stood up awkwardly at the bottom of the linen box and made it impossible to lay anything flat.

'Oh, Magda, for goodness' sake,' Stefanie said crossly. 'What is that?' She prodded the package with her finger. 'It's all bumps. Take it out. I can't get my nightgowns in. They will be all crumpled up.'

'It's Andreas' letters,' Magda muttered. 'And his portrait, which he gave me before he went away, and a piece of his hair in a bracelet, and—and one of his gloves he left behind!' Magda sat down on the floor and howled.

'Oh, Magda, don't cry! Oh, dear, I'm so stupid,' Stefanie tried to console her sister.

'I'll take them all out . . .' gulped Magda indistinctly.

'You shall do no such thing. We shall take them all to Moravia, even if it means throwing my nightgowns out of the carriage window on the way. Only don't cry. Just think, we may even see Andreas if he is still at Olmütz. We shall not be so very far away.'

Magda cheered up and the packing continued. The Captain could hardly have been unaware of their activity, but he seemed busy about some affair of his own. She glimpsed him once, hurrying towards his room with a long cardboard tube under his arm. His manner seemed secretive, and she was sure he had not meant her to see him.

'Joachim,' Stefanie said in the early afternoon. 'Is something wrong with one of the stoves? There's a dreadful smell of burning.'

'It's not the stoves, *gnädiges Fräulein*—it's that

French devil smoking the place out with his cigars. I told him he had no business filling your gracious lady mother's house with tobacco smoke and fumes, but he told me to be off, in no uncertain manner, and I'm not going to argue with a man who's nothing but a trained killer. He's been shut in that room since he came back today, after going out.'

'How very odd . . .' Stefanie said thoughtfully. 'What can he be doing?'

'He's studying that map, if you ask me,' Joachim said darkly.

The cardboard tube. Of course. A map. What else? She did not want Joachim to think he had told her anything of importance, so she said sternly, 'The Captain is our guest, Joachim, even if he is a Frenchman. You ought not to refer to him as a "trained killer". It isn't true, anyway.'

'Then what is he? I'll call him by his rightful title! You're a young lady and know nothing of such things. But I am an old man, and I've seen such men as that before! You think he is as you see him here, but if you were to see him at his trade, you'd think differently!'

'Be quiet, Joachim!' she said angrily. She waited until he had gone, and then, glancing about her to make sure no one saw her, tapped on the Captain's door.

'Come in!' shouted his voice, somewhat fiercely.

Resolutely ignoring the fact that going into his room was possibly the very last thing she should do, Stefanie pushed open the door and stepped inside.

A blue haze confronted her, and swirled into her nose and throat, making her cough. Through it, a shirt-sleeved figure could be seen bending over the table.

'Ah, the smoke,' he said. 'You don't like it. I'll open the window. Come on, come in and close the door.' It was something of an order.

The map lay spread out on the table, weighted at each corner to keep it flat by an assortment of objects including a shaving brush, one spur and a bottle of beer.

'Come and see,' he said. 'I did not mean you to see it, but as you're here, you'd better take a look. The old man told you of it, I suppose.'

'You've made this place look like company head-quarters,' she said accusingly.

'Not quite. You're forgetting the feather bed—the Army doesn't run to those.'

She *had* forgotten the bed, and the sight of it, in a somewhat higgledy-piggledy condition, since he had presumably denied the servant access to make it, re-minded her forcibly where she was. She sidled cautiously round to the far side of the table, away from him.

'What do you think?' he asked. 'I got this map in a bookseller's this morning, after I'd walked all over Vienna looking for a bookseller. What's the matter with you people? Don't you read? Do you do nothing but eat, sleep, dance and make love? In Paris there is a bookshop on every corner.'

'This isn't Paris,' she said, feeling her eye drawn irresistibly to the rumpled pillows on the far side of the room.

'No, your Emperor Franz is afraid of Revolution, I dare say. Too many dangerous ideas in books!'

'Put that cigar out!' she said crossly, pointing to the smouldering end resting in one of her mother's most expensive porcelain saucers.

'You put it out. I'm trying to rule a straight line.' He bent over the map with a pencil and a wooden rule and busied himself.

Stefanie picked up the cigar butt distastefully and dropped it out of the window.

He gave a grunt of satisfaction and put down the pencil and rule. Stefanie bent over the map and read out two or three of the place names.

'Why, this is mostly Moravia! You did believe the gipsy, you did!' she cried.

'I do *not* "believe the gipsy". Is this map correct, do you think? What an unpronounceable set of names. Why do they all end in -witz?'

'I suppose it's correct. I don't know. Anyway, as an Austrian, I shouldn't tell you.'

'Ah, we are back to that again, are we? Where's your country place on this? Don't tell me that's a military secret.'

'Here,' she said defiantly, and put a finger down on the map. 'Why have you ruled a line through Pressburg?'

'Just experimenting.'

'What are all these numbers? They look like arithmetic.' Stefanie picked up a piece of paper from the table top.

'That, mademoiselle, belongs to me!' He plucked it deftly from her fingers and pushed it into his pocket.

'Léon, something is going on,' she said earnestly. 'What is it? What's happening?'

'So, I've progressed to "Léon", have I? I'm not "Captain" any more.'

'Oh,' she flushed. 'I didn't mean it. It was a slip of the tongue.'

'A very nice one.' He rolled the map up smartly and pushed it back into its cardboard tube. 'And what can I do for you, mademoiselle? What caused this social call on me in my bachelor quarters?'

'I shouldn't be here. I only came to see the map.'

'*I'm* not the spy, *you* are!' he said.

'I'm not spying. I only want to know what's happening.'

'Oh, Woman, Woman . . . more curious than a cat! When you were small, did your nurse not tell you warning tales of inquisitive little girls whose noses turned into turnips and such like?'

'You don't mean to tell me?'

'I do not.'

There came a sharp knock on the door and Joachim's voice calling, 'A letter has been delivered for you, Captain. Official. Shall I bring it in?'

'What does he want?' Léon whispered.

'He's got a letter for you. He mustn't find me here —he'll tell Mama!'

'Good heavens, and ruin my reputation!' he said.

'Léon, don't joke. It's serious!' She began to panic.

'Pah! Hide in the wardrobe, then, if it makes you happier.'

Stefanie needed no second bidding. She wrenched open the wardrobe door and scrambled inside in an undignified way, pulling the door to after her. Inside, she crouched on the floor in the darkness. Some garment hung over her head and she was sitting on his boots. The interior of the wardrobe smelled of horses and leather and saddle soap. It was a nice, masculine smell and, unashamedly, she liked it. Through the door, she could hear movement in the room and voices. Suddenly, to her dismay, something long and heavy became dislodged and fell forward, striking her a sharp blow on the shoulder. She seized the object in her arms and clasped it to her bosom, just in time to prevent it crashing against the wardrobe door. Why was Joachim taking so long? Why didn't he go?

But he had gone, at last. A tap came on the wardrobe door, followed by a voice suffused with laughter.

'You can come out now, my dear. Or have you suffocated in there?'

The door swung open and Stefanie stepped out, still clasping the object to her.

'Do you mean to defend yourself against me with that?' he asked, pointing.

Stefanie glanced down. She was clasping a fearsome cavalry sabre in its scabbard. With a little cry, she threw it on the floor where it landed with a clatter.

'Treat that with respect,' he said. 'I paid a lot of money

for it, and it's all that keeps me in this world, and out of the next.'

'And dispatches others to meet their Maker!' she said vehemently.

'Well, we all have to go in the end and render accounts. How are your sins? Few in number, I'm sure. Mine would fill a book. As you are here, and Joachim has gone and will not "tell Mama", we could spend a pleasant half an hour adding another chapter.' He twitched an eyebrow and glanced at the tumbled bed.

Crimson, she retorted sharply, 'I shall do you the courtesy, Captain, of pretending I didn't hear that!'

'A pity,' he said regretfully. 'Ah, well. Listen, *ma chère*, whilst I was out this morning, I bought tickets for the theatre tonight. I particularly want you and little Magda to come with me.'

'Yes, if you wish. What's playing?'

'Oh, just a moment. I put the tickets in my breeches pocket. Here we are. They give Mozart, *Zaub—er —flöte* . . .' He stumbled slightly over the German name. 'I believe that is *The Magic Flute*.'

'I'll tell Magda.' She backed out of the room cautiously. But, with her hand on the doorknob, she paused and asked curiously, 'Tell me, what if I had agreed to your suggestion?' She pointed at the bed. 'Would you really have—I mean, here, in my mother's house . . .'

'Of course I should,' he said calmly. 'And if you linger here much longer, I might take advantage of such a splendid opportunity, anyway.'

As Stefanie fled, she heard him chuckle.

CHAPTER
SEVEN

To Stefanie's eye, the auditorium of the theatre seemed less crowded than usual, and every other man appeared to wear a French uniform. The normally fun-loving Viennese, awoken to cold prudence, were not venturing out at night. The theatre managers would happily have closed down their premises for the duration of the occupation, but the government had sternly decreed that all places of entertainment must be kept open, even if chiefly for the benefit of the French.

She knew the music well, and *The Magic Flute* was a favourite work, but she found it hard to concentrate on either Papageno's antics or the ingenuity of the scene-setters. Magda also looked distracted and complained frequently of the heat. In the first interval, Léon made an excuse and went to speak to a couple of brother officers.

'Why did he want us to come tonight, so particularly?' Magda asked querulously. 'It's so warm in here. I feel I shall faint.'

The heat from the forest of candles above their heads was certainly very uncomfortable.

'I don't know. He said something of our leaving for Moravia. It's a sort of treat, I suppose, for us.' Stefanie was watching Léon's conversation with the two officers. She could not hear what was being said, but all three appeared animated and to be arguing fiercely. Their earnest looks belied the occasion. Whatever they discussed, it was not Mozart.

'I wish we might go home. I don't like to be amongst so

many French uniforms. I feel disloyal to Andreas,' Magda complained.

'Then you should have refused to come,' Stefanie said sharply. 'What do you think they discuss so earnestly?'

'I did not want to offend Monsieur de Vaudry,' Magda returned irritably. 'But I've had enough, and I want to go home. I think they are only chatting—the French always wave their arms about like that. It means nothing.'

'Are you ill?' Stefanie gave her sister a close look.

'Only very warm and a little dizzy.'

But by the second interval Magda was complaining that her head swam dreadfully, and they were obliged to leave the theatre and take her home, after all.

'I'm so sorry,' she muttered contritely. 'I did not mean to spoil the evening. But I feel so faint.'

'Your sister is not well,' Léon said to Stefanie in a low voice. 'She has probably taken a chill. Help her to bed.'

Stefanie helped Magda to undress and get into bed, and then went to the kitchen and sought out the remainder of the wine they had drunk at dinner. She carried it back to the drawing room together with two glasses and put it all on a little table.

Léon, watching her in silence, said now, 'To what do we drink?'

'Not to anything. I thought you would like a glass of wine. I'm sorry about this evening. So is Magda.'

'No matter. I hope she is better tomorrow. We should not have taken her out.'

'Mama has gone out too, I think.'

'Aha, a little supper *tête-à-tête* with von Letzberg?'

'Don't speak so. You know I don't like it.'

'I apologise.' He stood up and went to pour the wine.

Stefanie sat down on a sofa and watched him. Something in his manner was different, but she could not pinpoint it. There was an earnestness behind his banter, and he'd never apologised before for anything. He had something on his mind.

'You like the theatre?' he asked, handing her a glass of wine.

'Very much.'

'You would like the theatres in Paris. I should like to take you to Paris, to see Talma play in *Mahomet*.'

'I might not be fashionable enough, perhaps,' she said demurely, sipping her wine. 'I lack a little of that Parisian *chic*, I'm told.'

'All the more reason to come to Paris and acquire it!'

'You have the worst manners of any man I have ever met,' she told him without rancour.

'I have long kept bad company.' He sat down beside her. 'You would not come with me to Paris?' His dark eyes held hers. It had come at last, the question she had read in them so often.

She put down her glass with a shaking hand. 'You are not serious, Léon?'

'Never more serious in my life, I swear.'

'You think I would—I would just go with you, when you ride out of here?' She heard the tremble in her own voice.

'I don't know. That is why I ask.'

'Oh!' she exclaimed, suddenly annoyed. 'It is preposterous!'

'Why?' With a swift movement he caught at her arm and pulled her round to face him. 'What is the matter with you, Stefanie? We are made of flesh and blood, you and I, not *papier mâché*. You act sometimes as though Eve never offered the apple to Adam! Of what are you afraid, for pity's sake? It is not a crime to be in love.'

'Is it love which makes you ask this?' she returned angrily. 'Let me go. How dare you make such a proposal to me?'

'To you? Do you think, then, I would ask such a thing of *any* woman? But I insult you, is that it? Well, you are a beautiful woman, my dear, and beautiful women are made to be loved! Don't look so horrified, mademoiselle,' he added drily. 'Men and women *have* been making love since the beginning of time. But perhaps you plan to pass through life pure and unsullied, like virgin snow? Possibly you think you would be defiled by my touch, or any other man's? But no, that is not how you feel, is it . . .?'

'Stop it, Léon, stop it!' she cried, putting her hands to her ears to block out his voice.

'No, I will not! Stopping your ears like that won't help you. You will listen to me. We have spent these last two weeks beneath the same roof, and you know as well as I what has been on my mind . . . and don't tell me it has never entered yours, mademoiselle—or that you have never wanted me to take you in my arms as I did that first evening—because I know better!'

White and trembling, Stefanie retaliated, wanting to strike at the roots of his self-confidence, 'Perhaps you do know better, Captain, with all the experience I dare say you have had! After an acquaintance of barely two weeks, I am supposed to surrender myself and my body to you, just as our army surrendered to yours at Ulm —one more trophy for the imperial eagles! Your path has no doubt been littered with such conquests. Where does love come into that? The rapidity and ease with which you dispense with normal preliminaries and courtesies makes it clear you have no time for any of those!'

'Of course I have no time for such things!' he shouted passionately, seizing her wrist as she would have jumped up and run away. 'Can't you understand? I *have* very little time! You are not indifferent to me. Don't pretend to me, and don't pretend to yourself! Would a little love between us be such a dreadful thing?'

'Léon, can't you see you ask the impossible?' she cried. 'Apart from anything else, you are French, I am a subject of Austria. Our countries are at war!'

'Nothing is impossible,' he retorted vehemently, 'you have only to want something enough! If you and I feel the same, then can we not make our private peace treaty? Must we two be at war also, because France and Austria fight? You spoke of the spoils of war. But I speak of the spoils of peace. If we are to enjoy those, we must do so *now*. Life never restores lost chances.'

'Léon, this is foolishness,' she replied earnestly. 'Earlier we spoke of my mother. Can you not imagine what such a thing would do to her? It would break her heart.'

'And it would not break mine, if you refuse me?' he asked gently.

She took a deep breath. 'Léon, please, I do not think your heart so easily broken. I accuse you of no insincerity—because I believe you really see nothing wrong with your argument. This—this desire for me, to you that *is* love. But love is not something to while away the time between campaigns! For you, Vienna is an interlude . . . like the music between acts in a theatre piece. Before you came here, your life was one of action—fighting, bivouacking. Now you find yourself in our beautiful city, in a comfortable house, leading a civilised life, visiting the theatre . . . Well then, what is more natural than a love affair to complete the picture? But when the time comes for you to leave, you will return to your real life, and your *real* love, and not need me. "There is no life like it", you said to me of the battlefield. I believe you. I cannot be a part of that life, Léon. I would just be in the way.' She smiled a little sadly at him. 'There will always be a pretty girl somewhere for you to take into your bed, Léon. It does not have to be me.'

'How wrong you are . . .' he said. There was a silence and then he gave a little shrug. 'Well, Léon de Vaudry, you are rejected!'

'Don't be bitter, Léon, or angry, please,' she begged, taking his hand, and afraid now, of what she might have done to this proud man.

'I am not angry, at least, not with you. There is enough of the gentleman left in me to accept your—your refusal with some grace.' He smiled at her, that crooked, disreputable smile that she loved so dearly, and it made her want to weep. 'You will not kiss me one last time, my dear? To show we do not part in anger?'

'I could not bear for us to part in anger, Léon. We do not see things in the same way, that is all. *I* cannot explain to you how I feel . . . *you* cannot understand.'

'You do me an injustice, *ma belle*. Come now, kiss me and we shall not quarrel any more . . . for if anyone were to hear us fling such hard words at each other, he would be convinced we *were* lovers!'

He reached out towards her and how easily she slid into his arms now. It seemed as if nothing moved in the house, no clock ticked, the world had ceased to spin and they two were one and must remain entwined in each other's embrace for ever in some infinite eternity.

'And you do not love me?' he whispered. 'Place your hand on your heart and swear you do not.'

She wanted to say 'I do not', indeed, knew that she must, but the words stuck in her throat. To pretend that she was not attracted to this man, as surely as the poor moth to the candle flame, would be to lie to herself. Like a magnetic force, the magical flame of a forbidden love drew her irresistibly towards it. Already she felt the burning heat of its destructive power as she was dragged into its beautiful, seductive and fatal orbit. She must not—could not—waver now; her resolution must not fail her. She and this man moved in separate worlds, towards separate destinies, and there was but one answer she could make him.

Yet how many reasoned arguments are destroyed in a moment by the simple touch of a lover's hand? Even as she formed her resolve, Stefanie felt herself weaken, and with a last concerted effort of will, she tore herself free from his arms and leapt up from the sofa. Backing away from him across the room, she stumbled into the table, and supporting herself against it, cried out in an agonised voice, 'No, Léon, no!'

Her words rang around the room, echoing in the crystal of the chandeliers, and followed by a deathly silence. 'Can you not *understand*?' she added fiercely. 'There can never be anything between *us*!' She struggled to calm herself, and continue in a forced, level tone, 'I shall go to Moravia with my mother and sister. You will stay here and, in turn, leave Vienna. When we return in the Spring, you will be long gone. Time will pass, and you will forget me.'

'*But I shall never forget you . . .*' whispered her heart.

As she finished speaking, he rose slowly from the sofa. She could not tell the effect of her words, for his face betrayed nothing. But when he spoke, his voice was more serious than she had ever heard it.

'Stefanie,' he said earnestly. 'About this journey to Moravia. I do not think you should go, none of you. I beg you to reconsider, not on my account—I would not presume to put forward such a reason—but on your own. I've already tried to reason with your mother, but she is a most obstinate lady. It will not be safe for unescorted women. There are soldiers of three nations tramping all over that part of your empire.'

'Wenzel, the coachman, goes with us,' she said, but he brushed this aside impatiently.

'Yes, I've seen Wenzel. He is built like a bear, and prepared to dash out anyone's brains in defence of his ladies. But it is not enough. Please, stay here in Vienna, at least until—' he broke off.

'Until what?'

'Until matters are settled,' he said obscurely.

'You mean until the next battle is won or lost. No, Léon, Mama will not stay. She will go, and Magda and I must go with her. We could not leave her to go alone.'

'You cannot know,' he said soberly, 'you have no idea. You think you will travel to your peaceful home. I fear you will find you journey into the mouth of Hell.'

'Are you sleeping, Magda?' Stefanie bent over her sister's recumbent form.

Magda stirred and mumbled something.

'What is it?' Stefanie put her ear to her sister's pillow.

'Andreas . . .' Magda muttered in her sleep.

'I would bring you Andreas, if I could,' Stefanie thought wretchedly. In the darkness of the bedroom, she stepped out of her petticoats, unwilling to light a candle of which the light might wake Magda. She could not help Magda. She could not help herself. She slid into bed and tossed uneasily on the pillow.

'I made the right decision, I told him the only thing I could tell him,' she thought.

'*I am going to make Captain de Vaudry fall in love with me,*' echoed her own voice in her memory, coming, it seemed, from centuries ago. '*And when he has, I shall reject him utterly . . .*'

How well she had succeeded in such an ill-conceived plan, and at what a cost to herself! It was all over and finished. A strange interlude, as crazy as a carnival escapade. The world was mad. It was full of blood and hate and combat. There was no place for Love, neither for her and Léon, nor for Magda and Andreas. The dogs of war were loose. Pursued by the devil's huntsmen, they led them all to destruction. These savage images whirled in her mind, until she fell asleep at last, a tormented sleep, filled with strange and fear-laden dreams.

She awoke, very suddenly. It was early, very early, a little before dawn. The room was quiet and still dark, but she felt the presence of someone—someone who stood by the bed.

'Who's there?' she whispered.

'Léon . . .' came the soft reply. 'Shh . . . be quiet!'

'You are mad!' She struggled to a sitting position. 'My sister sleeps here with me . . .'

'No, no!' He reached out in the darkness and took her shoulders. She could feel the touch of his hand against her skin through the thin material of the nightgown, and the warmth of his breath on her face. 'Listen, Stefanie, I am leaving now—'

'Now?' she asked, bewildered.

'Yes. I would have told you last night, after—well, after our conversation. But I have a morbid fear of goodbyes and, as you cannot come with me, I thought it best to slip away quietly. I have received my orders. It is possible we shall not meet again, and I found that, after all, I could not leave without saying farewell.'

'But, Léon—' She reached out and her hand touched the buttons of his coat. She felt for his face and her fingers brushed the cold metal of the brass dragoon helmet. 'Yes,' she said numbly. 'You are going . . .'

'Goodbye, my dear . . .' His hands trembled slightly on her shoulders as he pulled her towards him. She felt his lips on her neck and the horsehair plume of the helmet brush against her cheek—and then he was gone, a figure briefly silhouetted against the dim light from the corridor.

She heard a distant door close in the house, and it seemed another had closed with it, in her life.

Magda stirred. 'What is it?'

'Nothing, nothing . . . go back to sleep.' Stefanie lay down, pushing back her long hair from her damp brow and, in the first grey light of dawn, the hot tears began to trickle down her cheeks, slowly at first, then faster, until she broke into uncontrollable sobs and buried her face in the pillows.

CHAPTER
EIGHT

'YES, *gnädige Frau*, he left early this morning, very early, just on dawn. I let him out of the house myself. His groom waited outside in the street with the horses and took his box. He left a letter for you, *gnädige Frau*, and regrets he will not see you in person.' Joachim handed the Baroness a note.

Stefanie, who had come out of her room, clad in a wrap over her night attire, to listen to Joachim breaking the news to her mother, leaned her aching head against the wall listlessly.

Her mother's fingers were busy breaking the seal of the letter. 'How very extraordinary. Captain de Vaudry has left us, Stefanie! He writes here that he received orders unexpectedly to leave. He thanks us for our hospitality, and hopes his presence did not inconvenience us. Indeed, he proved a most charming and entertaining guest. If only we had known yesterday that he intended leaving. I would have had Cook pack a hamper for him. He may be a Frenchman, but I would not have him go hungry.'

'He took a loaf of black bread, *gnä' Frau*, and a ham sausage,' Joachim informed her.

'A ham sausage? Is that all? Why did you not give him the cold fowl? We hardly touched it yesterday.'

'It's all he would take, *gnä' Frau*. He said he would not plunder the larder.' Joachim hesitated. 'I gave him two bottles of wine. I thought you would not object.' Joachim fixed his eyes on the wall opposite and looked embarrassed. 'Two bottles of the Tokay, *gnä' Frau*.'

'The Tokay!' Stefanie cried angrily, stung out of her depression. '*Now* you give him the Tokay? You could not have surrendered it before?'

'He didn't need it before,' Joachim said obstinately. 'But it seems to me, when a man rides off to die, he might as well take a bottle of good wine with him.'

The room and its contents waltzed madly around Stefanie. She turned and ran back into her bedroom, slamming the door and leaning back against it, panting. Oh, why could even Joachim have understood what she had failed to understand? Léon's voice rang in her ears. 'I *have* very little time . . .' How passionately, how earnestly he had said those words, and how she had misinterpreted their true significance. He had not meant he had but little time in Vienna: but that possibly he had but little time to live. That the next great battle might count him among the fallen, or even before that, the next skirmish, a sniper's bullet, a foot caught in the stirrups of a drowning horse, floundering at the next river crossing. The bold adventurers who rode in the wake of their Corsican master, like great magnificently plumaged birds of prey in their fine uniforms, rode out to conquer or die beneath the imperial standards. Their confidence, their carefree attitude only disguised that they lived each day as if it were their last. Each day Death rolled the dice, and called some of their number to ride in the ghostly squadrons of his retinue. Those who survived, lived with an intensity they alone could comprehend, because tomorrow . . . tomorrow it might be Léon's turn, Léon, who had survived, incredibly, for almost eleven years as a Dragoon, who was a veteran of Marengo . . . whose luck must surely, one day, run out.

'And I had not the courage to match his,' she said aloud, dully. 'I could only list reasons why I could not love him. I had not the courage to take the hand he held out to me and say, "Yes, if it is only for a week, a month, a year—so that if Death comes for you, then at least you will know that I was yours, and I, too, could say, "I had your love, not even Death can take it from me".'

Magda was struggling to get out of bed. 'What is happening?' she demanded feverishly. 'Why do you look so wild?'

Stefanie ran to forestall her, bundling her sister roughly back onto the pillow. 'Stay there, Magda, stay in bed. Mama has sent for Dr Meyer.'

'I had such a strange dream,' Magda said. 'So odd. I dreamed I saw Captain de Vaudry standing by the door, only he was all dressed up with his helmet and sabre, as if he rode out to war—and I even seemed to hear his voice.'

'You were delirious. Lie still.' Stefanie hesitated. 'The Captain left this morning.'

'Without saying goodbye? Even to you, Stefanie?'

'Without saying goodbye—even to me.'

'I don't understand,' Magda said.

'No, neither did I.'

The doctor's opinion was, as the Baroness had expected it would be, that Magda's illness was due to nervous exhaustion. The suggestion that the journey into Moravia should be delayed on this account, however, threw Magda into an even worse state.

'We must go, we must! I know I may not see Andreas, but at least I shall be nearer to him. He knows we are due to arrive there any day now, and he may have sent a letter to the country house.'

Reluctantly, the Baroness agreed they should leave as planned. Magda, wrapped in furs, was settled in a corner of the carriage. On the floor of the carriage stood a large blue-glazed earthenware 'stove', resembling a huge vase with a lid, holes pierced around the top. Packed with hot coals, this contrivance filled the interior of the carriage with noxious fumes and overpowering heat, in which, besides Magda, the Baroness, Stefanie and Mitzi the maid must travel. Luggage was strapped on everywhere possible, so that they feared for the springs, and Wenzel, surveying the ready equipage gloomily, observed: 'Say your prayers that we do not get stuck in ruts, gracious ladies, for the horses won't be able to pull us out, not without unloading the lot!'

Hofrat von Letzberg, calling to wish them safe journey, advised them that the arch-fiend Bonaparte was in the neighbourhood of Brünn, and recommended them strongly to give that city a wide berth. The skies were clear when they rolled unevenly out of Vienna, but as they progressed onwards, the weather began to deteriorate. It became very cold, and the portable stove proved its worth. The sky became grey and cloudy, a steady drizzle began to fall, turning to sleet, as the night drew in.

In all, a wretched journey, on a road encumbered with French units, marching briskly along, despite the foul weather, sometimes singing snatches of popular songs, and exchanging robust banter. Besides his pack, each man was hung about with bought, bartered and stolen provisions. Pieces of pickled pork and slabs of bacon dangled from belts and musket barrels.

Late that evening, they drew into the yard of a small inn, overflowing with French uniforms. The bad-tempered and surly landlord at first swore that the French officers had taken all his available accommodation. Eventually, no doubt considering that the Austrian party would at least pay its bill, he offered them one miserable ill-appointed room. Stefanie looked for Léon, in the forlorn hope that she might glimpse his tall figure in the light of the inn's flickering lanterns, but in vain. They were glad to retire to their shared room, where they bolted the door securely, and tried to settle to sleep. Outside in the corridor, Wenzel rolled himself up in a blanket, just to make sure no one tried to disturb his ladies.

They need hardly have worried. No one seemed to have time to pay any attention to the four women. All night long, the high road echoed to the clatter of hoofs and the tramp of feet. Before dawn, just as Stefanie had drifted into some kind of restless slumber, a shrill whistling and whooping from the road, followed by cries of 'Stand clear!' in French, the thunder of hoofs and an immense rumbling, clanging and rattling, awoke her with a start of terror. It seemed some monster was rushing past, shaking the very building to its foundations.

By the dim light of a spluttering end of tallow candle, she saw that her mother was standing by the window, peering down between the slats of the shutters, and she slipped out of bed and ran across the bare wooden floor to join her.

'What is it, Mama? What was *that*?'

'An artillery train,' the Baroness whispered. 'They are moving up the heavy guns. But where do they go?'

Beneath their window, torches flickered and illuminated in their pitiless yellow glare, the faces of the men of one of the infantry regiments of the line, their faces grim, no banter now, marching resolutely in formation.

With a clatter of hoofs, a small detachment of Dragoons rode by, the infantry parting mechanically to let them through. The torchlight gleamed on helmets, spurs, buckles, bridle bits and sabre hilts . . . but the faces themselves were the faces of strangers.

'He has perhaps already passed this way, but I shall never see him again,' she thought in dismal resignation. And if he were to ride by? If she could fling open the shutters of her window, and call down, and see that battered, handsome, cynical, dearly loved face look up in the torchlight, what would it help? It was too late, all too late.

The Baroness turned away from the window and

touched her arm gently. 'Go back to bed, child. You will catch cold, and we must be ready to leave at first light.'

It was fortunate that they had brought food with them and could breakfast hastily and uncomfortably from their own provisions the next morning, for the inn could offer them nothing. The French had taken everything which could be eaten or drunk. A little hunchback schoolmaster, seated gloomily by the inn's stove, reported in tones of genuine anguish that the devils of Frenchmen had even taken away the few books of his little private library. Only the French, thought Stefanie, would take not only food, but books.

They had scarcely set off before they found they must again share the road with the marching infantry. The men formed two columns to the right and left, the horse traffic moving in the centre of the road between the two. The Baroness and her family found that they must travel at the pace of the French army, and not at their own. The pace of the columns was remarkable for its speed, and it was as if they were borne onward on a tide. Once, when Wenzel slowed the horses and would have rested, an artillery officer galloped up, shouting and swearing, ordering them to keep moving so as not to impede the advance of the great guns. In his wake came again that terrifying rumble and jingle. The marching soldiers threw themselves to the side of the road, and one of the great monsters drawn by its team of four sweating horses, drew alongside the Baroness' carriage.

'Good day to you, Ladies!' shouted the driver with a gallant flourish of his shako. 'Make way for Célestine!'

'Who is Célestine?' called Stefanie through the window, wondering if they were about to make the acquaintance of some particularly popular *vivandière*.

'Why, this is Célestine!' cried one of the gunners who trudged beside the great gun, and he patted the dull yellow-brown painted metal. 'The best wife a man ever had. She has a loud voice, but a sweet temper, and does her work well, eh, lads?'

The driver whistled to his team, and Célestine and her attendants rumbled past them and out of sight.

Some of the infantrymen had caught sight of the women in the carriage and began to whistle and call out compliments, not all of them decent, so that the Baroness pulled down the blinds and called to Wenzel to drive on.

After some minutes of semi-darkness, the gloom was so oppressive that the blinds were let up again, and the leaden light flooded into the carriage. It had begun to rain again, an icy, cutting, steady downpour, soaking the clothes of the trudging men.

'Poor fellows,' remarked the Baroness. 'Do they always march at such a pace?'

Stefanie had been wondering about this, too. It seemed to her that an air of haste and urgency hung over the marching columns. Officers rode up and down, alternatively encouraging their men and cursing them, always urging them to greater efforts.

Suddenly the carriage gave a lurch and halted abruptly. Stefanie, and Mitzi beside her, fell forwards, almost onto the portable stove. Stefanie seized at one of the hanging straps to steady herself, and put her head out into the misery-laden sleet to see what was amiss.

It was Célestine, at a crazy angle, wedged into a ditch. Her four horses strained and struggled, slipping to their knees in the mud, as the gunners pushed, heaved, hauled and cursed. Célestine would not budge. The artillery officer galloped up and began to yell instructions and some of the infantry came to lend their aid in the struggle.

Above her head, Stefanie heard Wenzel utter an oath. Then the coachman cracked his whip and without warning, the carriage leapt forward and set off at a breakneck pace, scattering the marching infantry to right and left.

'Why, whatever is the matter with Wenzel?' cried the Baroness. 'Does he want us to turn over? He will break all our necks. We shall finish like the gun, in the ditch!'

The carriage plunged on wildly and the four occupants hung on desperately, as best they could. At last Wenzel slowed the pace and eventually halted, jumping down from his seat to appear at the carriage door, his hat and whip in his hand.

'I beg your pardon, *gnädige Frau*. I hope, dear ladies, you weren't hurt, but I had to get us out of there! They couldn't shift that gun, not without extra horses, and I saw that officer look at *ours*, so I whipped up before those French devils unharnessed us and took our carriage pair. We shouldn't have got them back. They would have left us stranded in the mud there, sitting in a carriage with no horses to pull it!'

'Of course,' the Baroness said gratefully. 'Thank you, Wenzel.'

They travelled on through a desolate and deserted landscape. Dark, unfriendly forest gave way to abandoned fields and empty farmyards. Everyone had fled before the advancing many-legged monster which tramped on remorselessly, devouring all in its path. From time to time a halt was called and the exhausted men would sink down into the mud and rest their heads on their folded arms. Sometimes the halt was long enough to allow the poor wretches to light some kind of fire from damp twigs and broken branches. But before long, the officers, drawn and haggard themselves, would re-appear, kick the tired infantrymen to their feet and the great caterpillar would set off again.

At one of these halts, the marchers caught up with a civilian vehicle, a wretched unpainted farm cart, loaded with possessions and drawn by a pair of muddy and ill-kept oxen. It was driven by a poorly dressed peasant, and a woman sat beside him, huddled in a shawl and nursing a shapeless bundle from which an occasional dismal wail indicated life. Two other little children with pale, set faces, were strapped atop the belongings in the cart, together with, incongruously, a wooden crate containing two scrawny hens and a cockerel. Probably because of their primitive and agonisingly slow means of transport, the family had not been able to move fast enough to escape the advancing French, and now they were trapped. Two infantrymen stood by the oxen and a third had scrambled up onto the cart and was busy cutting loose the crate of poultry. The fowls squawked and fluttered, sensing their destination was the soup pot, but the children only sat and watched in apathy. The peasant who drove also seemed resigned to losing the last of his wretched livestock, apart from the oxen, and sat dejected on his seat. Only the woman protested. She stood up, clasping her baby with one arm and gesticulating wildly with her free hand, supplicating the soldiers not to rob them of one of the few things of any value they had left.

Wenzel drew up, and Stefanie heard him mutter, 'Bad business, bad business . . .'

The two infantrymen by the oxen, understanding nothing of the impassioned pleas addressed to them in Czech by the peasant woman, suddenly began to laugh and to imitate her Slav speech.

That was too much for Stefanie. She threw open the carriage door and, before her mother could stop her, jumped down into the mud. Running up to the oxcart, and heedless of the wind and driving rain, she shouted furiously in French, 'Cowards, cowards! What kind of men rob poor people like these? Don't you see how little they have?'

Wenzel gave an exclamation of alarm and hastily hitching the reins, scrambled down from his perch and ran up to protect his young mistress from the soldiers, who had stopped laughing and began to look sullen and vicious.

A dangerous situation had developed. Wenzel tugged at Stefanie's arm. 'Come, Fräulein, we can do nothing, come back!'

'Let me go!' she told him. 'I will not let them rob these poor wretches!'

The infantryman atop the cart had succeeded in cutting loose the crate and jumped down with it into the mud. The two children now began to cry, and the mother to wail despairingly.

'Put that back!' cried Stefanie at the soldier with the crate, beside herself in her rage, the more so because she knew she could do nothing to prevent his actions.

'You mind your own affairs, mademoiselle!' said the soldier insolently.

'Eh, Michel!' yelled one of the two who stood by the oxen, 'there's plenty of boxes and bundles on that carriage! Perhaps they can spare us a bottle or two of wine to wash down our dinner, or some fine white bread? Let's take a look!'

The next five minutes would almost certainly have seen the carriage stripped bare, but at that moment there came a shout and the thud of hoofs. Looking up, Stefanie saw, bearing down on them, a Dragoon officer, the horsehair plume of his leopard skin bound, brass helmet flying. He had drawn his sabre, and was brandishing it in no very friendly manner. The soldiers leapt back as he galloped up, afraid of being felled by a blow from the flat of the glinting blade. The two by the oxen melted away, and only the one with the crate was left standing by the cart.

A trooper of Dragoons came cantering up to join the officer. 'What's the matter, Captain de Vaudry?' he shouted.

'Léon!' Stefanie shrieked.

The officer sheathed the sabre and swung down from the saddle. His face was hard and unsmiling.

'Get back in that carriage!' he ordered her curtly.

'Oh, Léon—I'm so glad you're here! That soldier is stealing those chickens, and that poor family has nothing else—'

'What does the soldier have?' he demanded, interrupting her discourteously. 'This is not the Imperial Guard—we have no wagon train to supply us! That soldier and others must provide for themselves, take what they can find.'

Stefanie's mouth fell open, and the soldier, seeing how things were going, called cheerfully, 'Thank you, Captain!' He hoisted the crate of fowls onto his shoulder and set off with it briskly.

'You will not stop him?' she cried disbelievingly.

'No, be grateful I was in time to stop him turning his attention to your belongings. Now, get—back—in—that—carriage!'

'Not at your orders, monsieur!' she retorted, anger boiling up in her. She had wanted nothing so much as to see him again, and now she felt as though he had betrayed her.

He did not bother with further argument, but throwing his arms round her waist, hoisted her inelegantly over his broad shoulder and carried her kicking and struggling back to the carriage, dumping her in through the door with scant ceremony. Then he saluted the Baroness and said, 'Good evening, madame. I am sorry to see you here. I had hoped you might have stayed in Vienna, or turned back before now.'

'Good evening, Monsieur de Vaudry,' said the Baroness as politely as if they had met at a ball. 'Thank you for rescuing us from an unpleasant situation.'

'It was a fortunate chance I came by. Another time might not prove so lucky. Keep a tight hold of your daughter. She has a quick temper and no sense!'

'And you have no moral sense, nor sense of justice!' Stefanie stormed at him.

He ignored her. 'I will leave this trooper with you as

escort, for as long as possible,' he said to the Baroness. 'If I can, I'll come back later and see how you fare.'

He saluted again, and remounting, exchanged a brief word with the trooper before riding off.

'Wretch!' cried Stefanie after him.

'Now, now, mademoiselle,' said the trooper placidly. 'You don't want to call Captain de Vaudry names. He's one of the best.'

'He does nothing to stop thieves!'

'Well now, mademoiselle, these men here, they're on campaign, not on a Sunday parade. A man can't march and fight on an empty stomach. If that soldier hadn't taken the chickens, another one would. *I* might have done—' he went on a trifle regretfully, 'if I'd come along in time. As for Captain de Vaudry, he'd share his last crust. I saw him myself, earlier today, give the best part of a ham sausage to one of the soldiers' wives who follow after, and who was sitting by the roadside unable to go any further . . . and I know that sausage was his breakfast and he went without.'

'Oh, *Léon* . . .' thought Stefanie miserably, as Wenzel whipped up the horses.

Darkness fell over the desolate scene and still the columns of marching men and guns moved inexorably onwards. As there seemed to be no place of shelter, the Baroness and her family moved on with them. Wayside inns and farms were barred and deserted, and they moved through a landscape which looked as though some plague had swept through it, leaving nothing alive. At last they stopped to eat an improvised meal of cold meat, and to consider their plans. Their trooper escort had bid them farewell, and they would miss his cheerful company.

'It's like this, *gnädige Frau*,' said Wenzel. 'If we make a stop for the night now, I'll have to stay awake anyway to keep a watch on the horses. It seems to me, begging your pardon, that we should keep moving as long as *they*—' he pointed a stubby finger at the figures huddled in the gloom around them, taking advantage of the brief halt which had been called, 'keep moving. We stop when they stop, we move when they move . . . Blessed if I can understand why they are all in such a hurry.'

'They *are* in a hurry,' whispered Stefanie to her mother. 'Where can they be going?'

'We shall do as you say, Wenzel,' the Baroness agreed.

The columns reformed in the late evening and trudged on through the night, and the Baroness' weary horses plodded on with them. It was not until almost dawn that a command to halt was passed down the lines and the exhausted men threw themselves down onto the frozen ground. Wenzel drew up the carriage at the edge of a damp and dismal wood. The sky was clear of rain for the moment and the stars could still be seen, but the wind was icy chill and in the East a faint greyness heralded the gloomy dawn.

As Wenzel busied himself unharnessing his horses, which stood with drooping heads and heaving flanks wet with sweat, the Baroness and Mitzi set about organising the interior of the carriage so that the women could sleep in it. Very little sleep had been possible on the jolting drive. Magda, however, was asleep already, curled up in a cocoon of furs.

Stefanie climbed down, wrapped a woollen cloak about her, and walked a few paces away to stretch her numbed limbs.

'Don't you wander off, *gnädiges Fräulein*' came Wenzel's warning voice, 'or we'll never find you.'

All around them, the fires of hastily improvised bivouacs flickered in the darkness, so that they inhabited a curious, half-lit, nightmare world, split by leaping flames as if so many devils prepared their cauldrons. From the fires came the murmur of French voices, and once she heard a woman calling, perhaps a *vivandière*

selling brandy, perhaps one of the ragged camp followers seeking her man amongst the shapeless bundles
which lay sleeping around the fires. The courage and
endurance of these wretched women astounded Stefanie, and had impressed her deeply. A pall of woodsmoke
hung above everything, scenting the air with its acrid
tang, and infesting clothing with a lingering odour.

Léon would come—Stefanie was sure of it—and he
did. A tall figure, approaching on foot and leading a
cavalry charger by the reins, could be seen making its
way from fire to fire, enquiring, flames gleaming on
helmet and stirrup irons.

'Léon!' she called. 'Léon—we're here!'

'Ah, there you are,' he said, coming up to her. 'I was
beginning to think I wouldn't find you.'

His voice sounded weary and, without speaking, she
held out her hands to him. He hesitated for a moment,
then taking her fingers, bent his head and raised them to
his lips.

'Where is your mother?' he asked quietly. 'I must talk
to her, and she *must* listen!'

Something in his tone sent a shiver of apprehension
through her, and she led him quickly to the carriage.

'Why, Monsieur de Vaudry!' exclaimed the Baroness.
'Here we are, as you see, as merry as a band of gipsies!'

'So I see, madame. I should like to have a word with
you, if I may.'

'Of course. Step up into the carriage. Maria-
Magdalena is asleep and will not overhear. Mitzi, go and
see if there is any water to be had.'

'I should like mademoiselle Stefanie to hear what I
have to say,' he said, clambering into the carriage and
taking off his helmet. His face was unshaven and mud
streaked. 'We have stopped to collect our infantry stragglers and those who have fallen out along the way,' he
went on. 'Soon the columns will be reformed and we
shall move on.'

'Already?' cried the Baroness in astonishment. 'But you will kill your own men with exhaustion!'

'Soon it will be dawn, and we shall have but the daylight hours left. We must be there before this evening.'

'Be *where*, Léon?' Stefanie asked.

But before he could answer, a deafening 'Boom!' sounded from up ahead. Wenzel's horses neighed shrilly in alarm. The sleeping figures were awake in an instant, reaching for shakos and muskets and shouting out to know what was happening. The effect was as though a hive of bees had been disturbed.

Magda awoke with a cry of terror and clasping her mother's arm, gasped, 'Cannon!'

'Do not be alarmed, mademoiselle,' Léon said to her soothingly. 'The cannon does not fire in earnest. It is a device to encourage the stragglers, a trick, if you like. They will think there is some engagement up ahead, and it will get them to their feet.' He turned back to the Baroness. '*Chère madame*, the cannon will be fired in earnest soon enough. I cannot stay but a few minutes. The Dragoons are some two miles down the road at the head of the column, and are likely to move off without me if I linger! I have no time to plead with you at length. In a few words, then, I must beg you to turn back, now, before it is too late. Or, at the very least, to proceed no further. Rest here in your gipsy camp, wherever this is. The devil alone knows the name of this place. It must be obvious to you that this is a forced march. We are the reinforcements the Emperor will sorely need within the next twenty-four hours. The Emperor himself with our army, the might of the Russian army with massive reinforcements, the Czar himself, your Austrian army and your Emperor Franz, in all some one hundred and fifty thousand men, are all encamped less than forty miles from here. *Madame la baronne*, even you must see that we are marching into battle!'

CHAPTER
NINE

'ONE hundred and fifty thousand men?' the Baroness repeated. 'Is it possible? It will be a great battle, monsieur . . .'

'One for the history books,' he said with an attempt at his old, disreputable grin, but his dark eyes remained sober. 'Think carefully, madame, and God speed you . . . I hope back to Vienna!'

'God speed you on your journey, Monsieur de Vaudry,' the Baroness replied as he climbed down from the carriage and took the reins of his charger from Wenzel, who stood quietly by. 'Though I cannot wish you success, yet I pray God may protect you.'

Léon swung up into the saddle. For a moment his eyes met Stefanie's then he saluted and rode off into the lengthening grey streaks of dawn.

'Well, Wenzel,' the Baroness said, 'what do you think? You are to drive us. The Captain says we are headed directly for a field of battle. Three armies are encamped less than forty miles ahead. If I am correct, that puts them in the neighbourhood of Austerlitz, and *that* might well put them very near to our destination. Are we to stay here, or turn back?'

Wenzel stamped his feet on the frozen ground. 'Well, *gnä' Frau*, if you'll permit me to be so bold as to give my opinion, it's this: Turn back to where? To Vienna? That's as far as going on. Stay here? We can't do that more than a day. No fodder for the horses, see? Besides . . .' Wenzel hesitated. 'Besides, *gnä' Frau*, if there's to be trouble at home, then I'd like to be there.

That's where I'm from, as *gnädige Frau* well knows. Those are my people. Now, I know this country like the back of my hand. I can take us over the back roads. Not a comfortable journey, mind, but we'll make it. The horses were in good shape when we left, and although they are tired now and they are hungry, they won't drop in harness, not yet. Wait until these fellows move on, then we'll move out behind them and turn off the high road as soon as possible.'

After conferring together, they decided to follow this plan. In the early morning, the lines of weary infantry reformed and set off again. They followed for a mile or two, and then Wenzel turned off onto a winding track across the fields, and gradually the columns of marching men were lost from sight.

'If Léon comes seeking us again, he won't know what's become of us,' Stefanie thought, as they jolted along. 'Perhaps he'll think we've turned back to Vienna. But, knowing Mama, he may well guess we have gone on!' It seemed unjust that with so much to occupy his mind, Léon had to worry about their safety too. Though soon enough he would have little time to worry over them, if what he had told them was correct.

The carriage lurched and bumped over the country tracks. It was no longer raining, even a little warmer than the previous day, but the track they followed was badly churned into ruts which sometimes tipped them to an alarming angle and gave Mitzi to cross herself and murmur prayers for their deliverance. As the afternoon light began to fade, the carriage gave a final violent lurch and stuck fast.

They all descended onto the frozen mud and surveyed it. Glancing about her at the deserted countryside and distant hills, Stefanie said doubtfully: 'This all looks somehow familiar. Where are we?'

'Not ten miles from home, *gnädiges Fräulein*,' muttered Wenzel crossly. 'And this had to happen. Never mind, nothing broken, I'll soon get us out.'

'At least it's a little warmer,' the Baroness observed.

'Be a thick mist later tonight,' Wenzel prophesied dourly.

Despite his optimism, he was not able to get them out. First of all they unloaded the larger, and then the smaller, pieces of luggage until eventually everything which could be removed from the carriage lay strewn about them. Wenzel put his shoulder to a back wheel and Stefanie pulled at the horses' heads, her feet slipping on the uneven terrain, but still the struggling beasts could not heave them free.

'Now what?' demanded Stefanie, plumping herself down exhausted onto the linen trunk, in the middle of a sea of bundles. 'It's getting dark. We shall have to walk home.'

'What we need,' Wenzel rumbled, wiping the perspiration from his brow, 'is a pair of stout fellows to put a shoulder to the back wheels with me, but there's not a living soul about here.'

'Someone's coming now!' Stefanie said, pointing.

On the horizon and approaching rapidly was a large group of horsemen.

'Get back into the carriage, Ladies,' said Wenzel quietly, 'and don't show yourselves till we see who these fellows might be. You too, Mitzi, my girl!' He picked up his driving whip and went to stand by his horses.

They could hear the thud of hoofs now. Suddenly, a swarm of wild looking horsemen broke about the carriage like a tidal wave. Huge men, clad in dirty kaftans and mounted on shaggy little horses which seemed dwarfed by their giant riders, they brandished their weapons in the air and wheeled and turned about the carriage and the island of luggage. The riders' hair hung in long locks beneath their fur caps, and they wore straggling moustaches which gave them an Asiatic appearance. It was as if the centuries had turned back and once again the warriors of the Golden Horde swept down upon their prey.

Stefanie took Magda's hand tightly in hers, and they cowered back into the corner of the carriage.

'Cossacks!' murmured the Baroness apprehensively. 'Let us hope they have an officer with them.'

'So these are some of our Russian allies,' Stefanie thought. 'These are some of the men Léon must fight.'

At that moment, a thickset, middle-aged Russian officer appeared and cleared a way to the carriage through the ranks of his men by the simple expedient of laying about him vigorously with his riding whip. At the carriage door he dismounted. His face was very red, less from cold or exertion, Stefanie suspected, than from alcohol. In bad-tempered and execrable German, he demanded to know who they were and where they were going.

The Baroness explained, and during the course of her speech, the officer removed his hat and showed signs of belated politeness and some curiosity.

'You saw no signs of the French on your way, Ladies?'

'Constantly, until early this morning. Mostly infantry, who were coming from Vienna.'

The officer chewed at his moustache thoughtfully. Then he said abruptly. 'Well, you're behind our Russian lines now, so I'll allow you to go on to your house. But you'd best make haste.

'We ask nothing better,' said the Baroness graciously. 'But, as you see, our carriage is stuck fast.'

'Oh, we'll soon have you out of there,' he said carelessly, and turning to his men, shouted some orders.

Four of the Cossacks dismounted and with good-natured grins, put their broad shoulders to the back wheels. Wenzel urged his horses to take the strain and the carriage lurched out of the mud at last.

'You'd best repack your luggage yourself,' the officer said in a practical voice, putting on his hat. 'If these fellows do it, half will disappear into their pockets,' and he struck with his riding whip at a nearby soldier whom he evidently thought had approached unnecessarily close.

'What a very odd man,' said the Baroness, when the Cossack patrol had galloped off. 'Still, he was very helpful.'

'He was very drunk,' said Stefanie censoriously.

'I was never so frightened in my life,' said Magda in a small voice. 'One of the Cossacks kept staring at me. He said something to one of the others, and they laughed. I didn't like the way they looked at me—and I didn't like the way they laughed.'

'We shall soon be home, my dear,' the Baroness said soothingly, but something in her voice caught Stefanie's ear.

'Mama was afraid, too,' she thought, and the realisation that her valiant mother had been frightened, made the fear hideously real. Léon had been right. They should not have left the safety of Vienna.

Almost total night had fallen by the time they reached their destination, and wisps of gathering mist had begun to float across the fields. The house was in darkness, but as they drew to a halt, the front door opened and the stocky form of Janko, the gardener, peered out into the night, holding a lantern aloft in one hand, and ancient blunderbuss in the crook of his other arm. When he saw who it was, he let out a yell, and came running clumsily towards the carriage. Behind him loomed the mountainous form of his wife, the cook, Hanka.

'Oh, dear ladies!' cried Hanka, bursting into tears of joy. 'We've been that worried about you! Janko said, "they'll not come", but I knew better. Just you come inside. I've got the stove going in the little sitting room, it's been going since yesterday, just in case you came. Here, you, Václav!' she continued, addressing Wenzel by the Czech form of his name, and bestowing a hearty kiss on him. 'Why are you gawping there? Bring the ladies' things indoors. Janko will give you a hand.'

'Yes, Auntie Hanka,' said Wenzel docilely.

'It always makes me laugh, when we're here, to hear Wenzel call you "Auntie Hanka",' Stefanie said, smiling for the first time that day.

'And isn't he my own sister's son? There, Ladies, see, it's nice and warm in here.'

'But, Hanka,' the Baroness exclaimed, looking around the room. 'Where is everybody else? Is no one here but you and Janko? And where are the pictures and the ornaments?'

'The servants have gone, dear lady. Everyone's gone, except me and Janko. The whole village is empty. There's nothing but soldiers to be found anywhere. Some are ours, but mostly they are Russians, and very light-fingered they are, too! So Janko and I, we took down the pictures and all the china and put it all down in the cellar behind the woodstack down there. As for the silver, Janko put that in a sack, and has buried it in his cabbage patch. No one will find it there!' Hanka beamed.

'Oh, *paní* Hanka, thank you, but you should not have stayed,' the Baroness sighed. 'I had no idea.'

'Why, we wouldn't go off and leave you to fend for yourselves, dear lady! Anyway, everywhere you go, it's soldiers, soldiers. They came yesterday, the thieving rogues, and emptied the hayloft for their horses, so what Václav will feed your poor carriage beasts on, I don't know. They were Austrians who did it, too, and should have known better. I told them so, but all they said was, it was being "requisitioned". Huh!'

'What about food for us, Hanka?'

'So far they have respected the house, dear lady, but not the chickens or the pigs. Every one has been "requisitioned"! But there is still plenty of flour, and we killed a pig and made sausages last month, so no one will starve. There are all the mushrooms I dried in the summer, and the peppers and the cucumbers I pickled. It won't be elegant dining, but there's enough.'

'Well,' exclaimed the Baroness an hour later after a dinner of bread and sausage. 'In the morning we shall see how matters stand. I cannot think we shall be in any danger here. We are behind our own lines, after all.'

Even as she spoke, there was a sound of hoofs outside the windows, and a voice calling for the house to 'open up!' They looked at each other in concern, and Stefanie went to the window and peered out cautiously between the heavy drapes.

'It's not the Cossacks again, is it?' asked Magda fearfully.

'No, but a small party of riders. I think . . . Magda! It's Andreas!'

It was indeed Andreas, who came into the room accompanied by two handsome young Russians. Magda flew into his arms with a cry of joy, and it seemed to Stefanie that all their trouble had been worthwhile, if it had at least made the reunion of these two young lovers possible.

'Dear Baroness,' Andreas exclaimed, as he kissed the Baroness' hand. 'A Russian officer came in from patrol an hour ago and said he had met with three Austrian ladies who had travelled from Vienna, so I knew it must be you. No one else would be so intrepid! I came just as soon as I could.'

'We are so pleased to see you, Lieutenant von Letzberg,' she told him with a smile of welcome. 'You have been much in all our thoughts.'

Andreas then begged leave to present his two companions, of which one was a splendid young Cuirassier of the Imperial Russian Horse Guard, whose eye lit on Stefanie with a roguish gleam of interest. The other Russian, a Hussar, wore his hair long and braided into numerous thin plaits about his face, almost like a veil.

This curious fashion, then common amongst Hussars, was, Stefanie knew, intended as an inadequate protection for the face against the savage slash of enemy sabres.

These elegant young noblemen kissed the ladies' hands and, speaking in the stylish, drawling French of the St Petersburg salons, professed themselves honoured, and overcome with admiration at the ladies' courage in travelling through territory occupied by the French army, whom they described as a horde of brigands.

'*Geehrte Frau Baronin*,' Andreas said. 'The Cossack officer told us that you reported some extraordinary troop movements to him—French infantry, coming from Vienna, and yet in this vicinity.'

'Yes, indeed, we travelled partly in their company.'

'But, *chère madame*,' the Russian Hussar protested courteously. 'Are you sure you are not mistaken? These men could not have come from Vienna, since your Austrians inform us that Napoleon has left the bulk of the forces entrusted to Davout there. Have they sprouted wings? Can a whole army corps march some eighty miles in a mere forty-eight hours? It is unheard of, impossible! Even for the French, from whom we are accustomed to expect the extraordinary.'

'Well, the French have done it!' said Stefanie. 'They said they were the reinforcements for the battle which is expected near here.'

The other Russian shrugged elegantly. 'It is of no consequence. A remarkable achievement, of course, but of no significance. Men who have been marched to exhaustion will be quite unfit to fight. The outcome of the battle will not be affected by it. Tomorrow, Ladies, we shall crush the French underfoot, like so many beetles!'

'I cannot bear to think of it . . .' Magda said tremulously, holding tightly to Andreas' hand.

'It will be over in an hour,' the young Russian assured her with a charming smile. 'We outnumber Bonaparte by three to two, and his troops are exhausted and half-starved, including those whose forced march you witnessed.'

'When we heard the news that Bonaparte had occupied Vienna,' Andreas said earnestly, 'you cannot imagine the despair that was in my heart! I was at Olmütz, and every day people arrived there who had fled from Vienna. I could not sleep for imagining you in every kind of danger.'

As he mentioned the occupation of Vienna, Stefanie chanced to see the two young Russians exchange glances.

'Why,' she thought, 'they *do* despise us! They think we surrendered ourselves into French hands without a fight.' She remembered the snatch of conversation she had overheard on the evening of the ball. 'Their officers are polite enough to one's face, but behind one's back . . .' It was true, these likeable young Russians, confident of their own superiority, considered Austria a defeated nation. She was surprised Andreas had not realised this himself, and then wondered whether, in fact, he had. His next words seemed to confirm this last suspicion.

'Tomorrow will be a day of glory for us,' he said enthusiastically, squeezing Magda's fingers. 'They will see how Austrians can fight. We shall be avenged!'

'We had a French officer billeted on us in Vienna,' Magda told him. 'A captain of Dragoons.'

'A Dragoon?' said the Horse Guard, with all the contempt of a crack cavalry unit for the hard-pressed and ill-considered cavalry of the line.

'Popinjay!' thought Stefanie furiously. 'I doubt this fine young nobleman has even seen a real battle. He has done nothing but display himself in his splendid uniform to the ladies of St Petersburg. He has won more hearts in boudoirs, than honours on the field!' Perhaps she was being unjust, and the young Russian was as brave as he was handsome, but his manner annoyed her so much, she no longer cared.

'It is unforgiveable impudence,' the Russian Hussar said now sententiously, 'that French ruffians should be billeted upon good families.'

Stung, Stefanie burst out, 'He wasn't a ruffian! And if Kutuzov and the Russian army had not retreated, the French would never have reached Vienna!' She bit her tongue to prevent yet more, and worse, coming out.

Both Russians stiffened and the Hussar turned noticeably pale.

'His Highness, Prince Kutuzov, was left with no choice but to withdraw, mademoiselle, after your Austrian army surrendered at Ulm,' the Horse Guard said firmly though not discourteously.

It was a neat thrust, and the four Austrians present felt it.

Andreas flushed brick red, and cried out impetuously, 'Monsieur! General Mack waited in vain for a whole week at Ulm for the Russians to come to the relief of his besieged forces!'

It was time for the Baroness to quickly undertake the role of peacemaker.

'Whatever the reason, monsieur, there was no army to defend our city, and we were obliged, therefore, to throw open our gates to the enemy. You cannot think we did this with light hearts! But would you have had us allow them to batter down our walls, destroy our fine buildings, reduce Vienna to smoking heaps of bricks and stones, when we could not defend it anyway?'

'Yes, madame, yes!' cried the Hussar, leaning forward and speaking with such determination and earnest, even passion, that Stefanie was astonished. 'You should have let Bonaparte destroy your city, even destroyed it yourselves! Torn down every building with your own hands! Set the city ablaze from one end to the other. Anything! Anything, rather than allow it to fall into the hands of the French. That is what we Russians would do. Let Bonaparte find his prize nothing but smouldering ruins! That is what we would do, if he were ever to threaten a Russian city.'

There was a silence.

'Vienna has survived the Turks,' the Baroness said gently. 'She will survive the French. Wars and generals come and go. But our city stands, and what she stands for, in our hearts, that will remain when all the fighting is done.'

The officers smiled and rose to take their leave, bowing politely.

'I shall come back, just as soon as it is all over,' Andreas promised Magda fervently, clasping her hand, as he stood up to leave with his companions.

'And lay the so-called "imperial standards" of the French at your feet, Ladies!' the Horse Guard added with an engaging grin, and Stefanie realised how very young he was, perhaps no older than Andreas.

'Boys led into battle by old men,' she thought suddenly, and her heart sank.

Exhausted by their journey, they retired to bed early. But after blowing out the candle, Stefanie went to stand at the window in her nightgown, although the room was very cold. She opened the shutters, and leaned her head against the window frame. Outside, little wisps of mist snaked across the ground, but between them, in the darkness, gleamed pinpoints of light, glittering as far as the eye could see, as if the stars had fallen to earth. They were the bivouac fires, around which ate, talked and slept men of many European nations, drawn to this place for a moment of colossal slaughter. In French and Polish, German, Hungarian and Russian, they joked and reminisced and argued. Many slept, rolled in blankets near to the welcome heat of the flames, but many felt no wish to sleep now, knowing only too well that after the morrow they might sleep for ever.

Near one of those fires, perhaps, Léon was standing, or was sleeping in some makeshift shelter. He was, quite possibly, no more than three or four miles away, over there, beyond the Russo-Austrian lines. She wondered whether he had time to think of her, whether he would ever have time again to think of her.

Stefanie turned from the window with a shiver, not only of cold, for the distant fires seemed suddenly full of an unseen yet hideously present evil. She crept back into bed and pulled the feather quilt up over her head to close out both the cold air and the threat which lurked outside in the gathering mists. It seemed impossible that she should sleep, but she dozed fitfully until about two in the morning, when she awoke suddenly with a start. She was aware of, rather than heard, a movement outside the house and, as she strained her ears, they seemed to catch the clip-clop of a hoof. Very, very faintly, she heard the murmur of voices below and now, certainly, someone was coming very cautiously and quietly upstairs.

Stefanie swung her legs over the edge of the bed and pulled a woollen shawl around her. Desperately, she wondered what she might use as a weapon to confront the intruders, and finding nothing else, took down a heavy ebony crucifix from the wall, trusting she would be forgiven if she were obliged to use it in her defence.

The door of her room creaked open to admit the flickering light of a candle, and, to her immense relief, the voice of Mitzi, the maid, who whispered, 'Fräulein? Are you awake?'

'Yes, Mitzi, what's wrong?'

'Make no noise, Fräulein. Nothing is wrong. The French captain is here. He's downstairs in the kitchen and—'

Stefanie did not give her time to finish. She dropped

the crucifix on the bed, and ran past Mitzi down the ill-lit stairs to the kitchen.

The open fire over which Hanka cooked was still burning, and someone had added another log which set the yellow flames crackling brightly, bathing the kitchen in a rose-gold glow against which the shadows leapt and danced with devilish merriment. The rows of copper pans gleamed on the wall as if turned to gold by the touch of an elvish hand.

Léon stood silhouetted against the firelight, a tall figure staring down into the flames which played across his hawklike features. As she flung open the door, he turned his head, the shadows fell across his face and in them, the dark eyes seemed haunted by some inner turbulence of soul. Then the shadows moved again, and the eyes rested on her with their vivid, piercing gaze.

'You did not expect me,' he smiled slowly, his disreputable, crooked grin.

Stefanie, who had stopped in the doorway as if transfixed, came slowly into the room, and held out her hands silently in welcome.

'I . . . how did you come here?' she whispered, finding her voice.

He glanced behind him to the back door and gestured vaguely towards the night. 'I came through the Russian lines,' he said simply, as if this were a matter of no great difficulty.

'You did *what*?' she gasped, hardly able to believe her ears. She reached out a hand and grasped his shoulder, so shaken was she by the sudden realisation of the dangers he had run. The words began to tumble out of her in a frenzied jumble. 'But it was madness! What if you were seen? What if you were captured? Suppose a sentry had challenged—'

'Don't be so alarmed,' he said quietly, smiling a little. He took her hand from his shoulder and brushed the tips of her fingers with his lips. 'No one saw me. I am no raw recruit, you know. I am wise to the ways of pickets and patrols. Besides, I had help.'

'Help? Who helped you?' she asked, bewildered.

'Not "who" at all—the weather helped me. Take a look out of the window. You'll see a thick mist is covering everything.'

'There are Cossack patrols out there,' she said fearfully, remembering those wild faces which had surrounded the carriage. 'Supposing *they* had found you?'

'I prefer not to think about *that*!' he said drily. 'And as for the risk . . .' he paused. 'I took it to see you. It seemed to me, it was worth it.'

'It was worth risking your freedom, even your life, just to see me?' She stared at him wildly.

He smiled and slipped his arms around her slim body, drawing her towards him, and she was so confused within herself that she could offer no resistance. But then his grip tightened around her and he buried his face in her thick blonde hair.

'Did you really think I would *not* come?' he murmured, and, lowering his head, he caught the tip of her ear in his lips.

At the touch of his mouth, she gave a nervous start. The blood began to race in her veins and she drew sharply away from him. He released the pressure of his embrace, and lifting his head, studied her face, his own sober.

'I did not see how you could come here,' she whispered hesitantly, for there was something written in those dark eyes which she could not read. 'Though I knew you would guess we were here. Léon—I looked out of the window earlier tonight, and saw the fires burning in every direction. I knew you were there, and I was so frightened . . . The peasants around here tell strange, old folktales—of mysterious valleys and rocks which move and reveal the entrance to the Underworld. There are places about here where no one will venture at midnight or at full moon. Tonight it was as if just such a cleft in the mountain side had opened, and I could look down and see into the fires which burn for ever, and all the little imps and devils were about to come dancing out and overrun everything.'

He did not answer her at once, but lifted his hand and began to stroke her hair softly. 'I have seen that sight many times,' he said at last. 'You must not lose heart now. They are only the fires of men, and not of goblins.'

He cupped his hands about her face and tilted it up towards his.

How strange, she thought, that one man's touch could be at times so gentle, and at others so violent. What a complex and passionate nature dwelt behind those expressive dark eyes which looked down into hers, and how little she understood it. She wanted to reach out to him, and yet she was afraid, afraid of the unknown corners of that nature. Yet there was something in him which cried out to her, too, something unsaid, unexpressed, perhaps inexpressible, something he could not say.

He spoke now, very quietly and earnestly. 'Listen to me, Stefanie, I did not only come to see you, but to act as my own courier. I wrote you a letter earlier this evening. It's here . . .' He delved into his coat and produced a rather battered piece of paper, folded and sealed. 'I apologise for its condition, and for the hand-writing, which isn't very good. I had no table or anything to rest it on, and had to rest it on my knee, and the firelight made it awkward, too. But it is a strange sort of letter in any case, for it is one I hope you will never read.'

'That I shall not read? You have taken so many risks to bring me a letter I am not to read?'

'If you like.' He took her hands in his. 'The thing is, no one knows how a battle will go. Whether we win tomorrow—no, it is no longer "tomorrow", it is already "today"—whether we win or not, as Fate decrees, I may or may not come through it myself. Don't look so

frightened, *ma chère*. I promise you, I shall do my
utmost to survive! I have no wish to quit this earth ahead
of my time, especially now . . . If things go well, then
trust me, I shall come back, and tell you what is in this
letter myself. If, for any reason, I cannot come . . . then
you will read the letter, and it will speak for me. If I don't
come, you will know it is because I cannot. Nothing will
prevent me from coming, if there is breath in my body, I
swear.'

She took the letter with trembling fingers. 'I
know . . .'

'You asked me,' he said quietly, 'if it was worth the
risk to come here. You should know that you are the
only cause which can make any action worthwhile for
me, and what you think of me, the only judgment by
which I set any store.'

'I . . . I will wait for you, Léon, and pray you will come
to tell me yourself what you have written here.'

'You'll see me, don't fear. I'll come, if I must cut my
way singlehanded through the Czar's entire army to do
it!' He bent his head to kiss her lips, at first gently, and
then with such a growing and insistent passion that,
knowing what he sought and fearing to yield to that
demand, she began to whisper, 'No—no—no . . .'

'Fräulein!' Mitzi, who had been keeping watch outside, ran into the room. 'I can hear riders on the road!'

'Put out the candle!' he said quickly, releasing
Stefanie abruptly and thrusting her away from him. 'Are
the shutters fast?'

'Yes, Captain,' Mitzi assured him. 'No one can see a
light from the road.'

They all held their breath as the clatter of hoofs
announced a patrol which passed by the house. Then, to
Stefanie's utter dismay, just as the danger seemed past, a
loud piercing whinny sounded from outside.

'Damn that horse of mine!' Léon muttered. 'It's calling to the others. I must stop it!' He wrenched open the

THE EMPEROR'S DRAGOON

back door and raced out into the night.

Stefanie ran after him, heedless of the bitter night air penetrating her cotton nightdress, and the frosty earth beneath her bare feet. Outside the kitchen door, she found she had plunged into a thick swirling mist. No longer could the stars be seen, or the bivouac fires, only a dense, clammy blanket which covered all. Although Léon was only a few paces from her, she could not distinguish him, and stumbled into him in the darkness and choking fog. He was holding the reins of his charger with one hand, and had clasped the other to the animal's nostrils to silence it.

'Go back,' he whispered urgently. 'Go back, you will catch your death of cold!'

'Do you think I care? Léon, how will you get back? How will you find your way in this dreadful fog?'

'Bless the mist, don't curse it. It hides me from the Russians and it hides me from our own patrols! If I fall in with them I'll have a devil of a lot of explaining to do! But don't worry, I've a pretty fair sense of direction . . . I'm used to blundering around blind in gunsmoke and filth. This is no worse and, you know, if it lasts, this mist, the Russians won't know where to look for us in the morning! I wonder . . .' He took his hand cautiously from the horse's muzzle, and slipping his freed arm around her, pulled her towards him and kissed her hurriedly. 'For God's sake, go back!'

He released her and swung up into the saddle, yanking round his horse's head. With a flurry of hooves, the darkness and swirling mist swallowed him up, and he was gone in a second, even the muffled hoofbeats lost to her ear.

CHAPTER
TEN

THE time, some hour and a half only, till dawn, could not be spent sleeping, and Stefanie returned upstairs, not to bed, but to dress herself and break the thin layer of ice which had formed on the pitcher of water on the bedside cabinet, so that she could wash her face. Then she brushed her hair, tied it back with a ribbon, and went downstairs to the warm kitchen again.

There, she sat on the wooden settle by the fire, staring alternatively into the crackling flames, and at the place where Léon had stood, as if some ghostly imprint of his presence was still there. Slowly the log on the fire was consumed. She watched it blacken and then turn grey and finally to white ash. It seemed as though it represented every secret wish hidden in her heart.

Stefanie leaned her head against the wall and closed her eyes. Despite everything, she must have drifted into uneasy sleep, for it seemed to her as if a thunderstorm raged. Half awake, dragging herself from slumber, she heard the thunder roll and was aware of the flash of the lightning. Then, all at once, she awoke and leapt up with a cry of fear, realising that it was not thunder, but the voices of the great guns, and the lightning was the flash of powder.

Magda's voice was calling out to her in terror, and she ran upstairs to her sister's room. Magda, still in her nightgown and with her dark curls tumbling onto her shoulders, ran to her barefoot and clung to her shrieking, 'What's happening?'

Stefanie went hastily to the windows and threw open

the shutters. It was morning, but outside it was still as dark and gloomy as at dawn, for the mist, thickened by the smoke of the hundreds of camp fires, hung above everything. Through it could be seen faint shapes, trees, fences, barns and stables. Suddenly, on the horizon, the grey veil was seared by a comet of orange and red. The air became alive with confused and distant sounds, the cries of men and the neighing of horses, trumpets and drums, the crackle of musket fire and above all, the bronze mouths of Célestine and her sisters, sending forth their messages of death.

The Baroness hastened into the room, fully dressed, and joined them at the window.

'Wenzel thinks they are as yet no nearer than four miles. But battles ebb and flow,' she said rapidly, 'and the engagement could come closer. We must be prepared for any eventuality. Hanka is taking food down to the cellar, and if necessary, we shall take refuge there. Maria-Magdalena, get dressed now. Quickly, child!'

Magda only stood as if frozen to the spot, at the window, seemingly unable to comprehend. Stefanie sought out her sister's clothes and dressed her almost as if she were a small child.

'If only the mist would rise,' Magda whispered as Stefanie struggled with the hooks of the gown, her fingers trembling nervously despite gritted teeth and a determination not to be demoralised by the distant uproar.

'It will, you'll see, in an hour or two the sun will break through and we'll be able to see what is going on. Perhaps, if we go up to the attic—I think there's an old spy-glass of Father's up there—we shall be able to distinguish some uniforms.'

'But how can they fire at each other in this mist? They could be firing at their own men.'

'*I* don't know. They are probably blundering around looking for each other.' She paused. 'Perhaps the cavalry will not go into action in such conditions.'

'Do you think so?' Magda seized on this. 'Perhaps they will call a cease-fire, if the mist persists.'

'They won't do that!' Stefanie said practically. 'They have gone into action and must fight it out. Put your shoes on and come downstairs.'

Between eight and nine that morning, the mist slowly thinned and lifted. The sun, after threatening to break through for an hour, sent its clear, pale winter light to bathe the scene. At any other time, it would have been a fine day for the season.

Their ears had almost become accustomed to the cannons' roar, the explosions, the whine of grapeshot and the shouts and screams borne towards them on the breeze. Stefanie and Magda climbed the stairs to the attic and from the topmost window of the house, they tried, with the help of the spy-glass, to identify the tiny figures which appeared and vanished in seeming wild confusion.

'There are a lot of men over there, towards Olmütz, in very dark uniforms. I think they are Russians. I can't see what they are doing, they just seem to be moving away.' Stefanie swivelled the spy-glass around. 'I can see cavalry!'

'Where? Let me see!' Magda seized the spy-glass from her. 'I can see them too, hundreds of them. But whose are they?'

'I don't know,' Stefanie retrieved the spy-glass and put it to her eye again. 'I think they are Cuirassiers, I can see the light reflected off their breastplates. There seems to be a thousand or more! Now they have disappeared over the rise in the land and I've lost them—oh!'

There was a deafening echoing explosion and the house shuddered. Without warning, a crack ran the length of the window panes and from below in the house somewhere glass shattered and crashed to the ground.

'They've changed their positions!' Stefanie grasped

Magda's arm and pointed. 'The artillery is firing over there, towards the lakes, look! They've come nearer!'

'It's impossible to tell anything,' Magda said dejectedly. She sat down with the spy-glass in her lap. 'One can't see who is winning.'

Win? Did that word have any meaning now? Whoever "won", either she or Magda must grieve with the vanquished, Stefanie thought.

'Those Russian officers said it would be over in an hour—that just shows how much *they* know!' Magda went on, twisting the brass telescope in her fingers. 'I don't believe anyone could survive out there. They will all be killed, all of them! No one could live amongst it. It's dreadful, horrible, devilish! Everything, everyone, must be destroyed.'

'The mouth of Hell . . .' Stefanie said quietly. 'He warned me of it—and I saw it, last night, open . . . and now all the evil has come out.'

She took Léon's letter from her pocket and turned it over in her hands. It was inscribed: 'To the honourable and gracious Baroness Stefanie Vezemsek.'

The writing was very crooked and the paper smeared with wood-ash. She imagined him, seated by the open fire in the freezing night temperature, the paper balanced on his knee, jostled by his comrades, the ink congealing in its pot from the cold.

'No one can survive out there, no one . . .' Magda repeated desperately as the cannon roared again and all the windows rattled. 'They must all be killed. Perhaps we shall be, too, if it comes here.'

He had run such danger to bring her this letter. He had wanted so much that she should have it. He could only have done that, because he believed he would never be able to come again in person. It was a last testament . . . the voice of a man who stood on the threshold of his last day on earth. She felt it with her fingers. It contained some small flat round object, like a coin.

'I hope you will never read it,' he had said of the letter, but she would read it, because even in the midst of battle she could, whilst reading it, be with him. She broke the seal, and spread the paper out flat.

'*Chère mademoiselle*,' it began, with an oddly dignified yet moving courtesy. 'No wish could be nearer to my heart that that your eyes should never read these lines, and that I could be there myself to tell you what I write and beg you to believe is true.

'I have no wish to live if it must be without you. The fear that you would continue to reject and despise me, has been the greatest fear that I have ever known. No cannon's roar, no enemy's aspect, has ever filled my heart with such dismay as that one thought, which has haunted my waking hours and invaded my dreams.

'I know I am, for you, a being of war, an enemy, an occupier of your home and your country. I am a part of that army which kills and maims your country's soldiers, reduces to rubble the homes of your citizens and lays waste the very soil which is the lifeblood of your peasantry. Yet is it not my fault if I come to you in this guise. God knows, I would have come to you in a gentler one, had I been able. Rather, it is Destiny which has brought me, and brought us to know each other, and, in happier times, would have brought us to love each other freely.

'I know well that there is so much in me—and what I represent—that you must abhor . . . that I am a man of blood, and not of peace, a creature of darkness, perhaps, yet one who struggles towards the light of your respect and your love. I have never loved any woman but you. No woman could ever take your place, no woman even be a shadow of what you are to me. If I am killed, and you read these lines, then know that I am better dead, and all is for the best, since I cannot know any happiness on earth without you.

'My dearest, I beg of you one favour, one request, that

you will carry out one small commission for me, in the event of my death. The gold medallion I enclose, was given to me by my mother many years ago. I have not been the best of sons, but I have kept her gift, neither losing it in battle, nor at the gaming table. I know I can leave it in no safer hands than yours, and beg you to return it to her—madame la comtesse de Vaudry at Epernay.

'Had I been able, and fortunate enough, I would have taken you to Epernay myself—have ridden out to war no more, but been content to grow old with you, watching the grapes ripen on the vines . . .

'If you cannot think well of me, at least, do not think badly.

'I kiss your hands,

' L. de V. '

Stefanie turned the medallion over in her fingers. It was of Our Lady, and attached to a thin gold chain. She folded it up in the letter again and put it all back into her pocket.

'What is it?' Magda asked listlessly.

'A letter, only a letter.' Stefanie roused herself. 'Don't despair, Magda. Andreas will be safe. You'll see. You must not lose faith.'

'No, of course not. I know he will come back,' Magda agreed, with brave optimism. 'But it is the waiting, and not knowing what is happening. Will the cannon never cease firing?'

The firing did not cease, but it did lessen considerably towards mid-afternoon. Wenzel, who had ventured out cautiously to see what he could discover, came back in haste.

'The troops are moving this way, *gnädige Frau*! Hundreds of them! If you ask me, things have not gone well for us. I saw no French, but any number of Russians, and half a squadron of Hungarian Hussars who looked as if they had been chopped to pieces.'

'Do you mean, Wenzel, the Allies are retreating?' the Baroness demanded.

'The Russians are dragging their guns along, *gnä' Frau*, or so it looked to me from where I was. The units all seem to be mixed up together, footsoldiers and cavalry. If you ask me, it's every man for himself!'

Magda gave a cry of distress, and Stefanie put her arm round her sister's shoulders. 'Wait, Magda, wait! If they are coming this way, we may be able to get some real news. Wenzel could be mistaken.'

They all ran down to the gate by the road and sheltering their eyes with their hands against the wintry sun, tried to see into the distance.

The horses came first. All her life, Stefanie was to remember the horses. Wild drumming of hoofs heralded them, and then they burst into view. Riderless, wet with sweat, caked with mud and smeared with blood, their nostrils flaring and their rolling eyes so white and staring it seemed they would start from the sockets, they plunged madly onwards. Empty stirrups flailed viciously, broken bridle reins threshed about them and the caked foam about their mouths gave them the appearance of rabid creatures.

At their head galloped a great black charger, with red saddlecloth edged with gold, and a sheepskin shabraque covering the saddle. So close did it pass to them, that Janko made to seize the loose reins which cracked like a whiplash about the animal's head.

Wenzel uttered an oath and leaping forward, grabbed Janko by the arm and dragged him back. 'Leave it, man, leave it! It is mad from the sound of the cannon and the smell of blood. Nothing can stop it now—it will run until the heart bursts and it drops in its tracks! It has been driven mad!'

Magda, white and shaken, whispered brokenly: 'That saddle harness—the red and gold cloth, the fleece shabraque—that belongs to an Austrian Hussar. They are

Austrian horses!' Her voice rose on a note of panic. 'But where are the riders?'

Men, mounted or on foot, singly, in twos and threes, or in semi-organised groups followed. Where now were the fine uniforms and handsome faces which had graced the ballrooms of Vienna and the palaces of St Petersburg? The uniforms were torn and slashed by sabres, holed by musket fire, burned by powder, streaked with mud and soaked in blood. The faces were those of men who had ridden out that morning in the flush of youth, and returned now, so few hours later, aged and bewildered.

No one could give them any news. No one had time to stop. The fear of being taken prisoner drove them onwards. The Russian infantry, demoralised and leaderless, did not understand their frantic questions, and a Hungarian Hussar, his blue dolman unrecognisable and his face swathed in bloody bandages, shouted at them as he clattered past: 'Get out of sight! Get those women out of the way!'

'Yes, Magda, Stefanie, come along now!' the Baroness ordered. 'You must get back to the house. Get down into the cellar and stay there. Hanka go with the young ladies.' She put a hand on Stefanie's arm and whispered, 'Take care of Magda. You understand *what* it is I fear for you both?'

'Yes, Mama,' Stefanie said awkwardly. 'But what about you?'

'If soldiers come and find me, they may seek no further. Go, go . . .' She pushed Stefanie after Hanka and Magda.

The cellar was bitterly cold and dank. It was also very old, older than the house built above it. Its vaulted roof was supported on massive pillars of stone, rising to pointed Gothic arches. The floor of beaten earth had a mouldering smell, like a crypt, and in one corner a stone rim marked the site of an ancient well, whose depth was an unknown mystery and which had been boarded over for safety. It was traditionally held that these cellars had once lain beneath a building, long since disappeared, half monastery and half fortress, dating from the days when the Teutonic knights had held sway here. Certainly, those feared warriors of mediaeval Christendom must now be stirring in their eternal slumbers at the sounds of battle which permeated even down here through the apertures pierced high up at ground level.

Stefanie and her sister, crouched in the gloom, could hear the tramp of feet as the numbers of retreating soldiers increased. Hanka, sitting on a cask, and clasping a plaster statuette of St John Nepomuk to her ample bosom, was muttering prayers. In a far corner of the cellar something fell down, and the sound was followed by a squeaking and a scattering of claws.

'There are rats down here!' whispered Magda, cowering against Stefanie.

'Don't be frightened,' Stefanie returned in a low voice. 'If we don't bother them, they won't bother us.' She wished she could believe the same of the retreating soldiery.

Time passed slowly. There was little sound of feet now, but from time to time the voice of the cannon was heard. Chilled to the bone, they emerged from the cellar and gathered in the kitchen to warm themselves. It was a curious moment, a little like the interval in a theatrical production. One set of players had come and gone, and they awaited the next. But what nationality would they be? Defeated Russians, frightened and desperate, or victorious French, flushed with success and seeking plunder and trophies?

'Andreas has not come,' Magda said in a very small voice. 'In another hour it will be dark.'

'Give him time, it's not over yet,' Stefanie told her.

'It *is* over. Austria and Russia are defeated. Andreas

promised he would come,' said Magda obstinately. 'He is dead or prisoner, I know it.'

'You do not know it!' Stefanie said sharply.

'Then where is he? He is dead—or dying, somewhere out there, with no one to care for him.'

Stefanie remembered the ragged train of camp followers whose tenacity had amazed her so. But now she understood those women, many with babies in their arms, who doggedly trudged behind the marching columns. For who else but a devoted heart would seek out the wounded soldier, of no interest now to his superiors if he could no longer fight—and care for him? Surgeons concentrated their dubious skills on the officers, and the defeated enemy was left to face the final agony alone. That might indeed be Andreas' fate. But Léon, too, might be out there somewhere, sprawled helpless and disabled in the mud, or lying on the bloodstained straw of the field hospitals, awaiting the butchery of the regimental surgeon.

'Wenzel,' she said. 'Do you think, you could put the horses to?'

'Why, where will you go, *gnädiges Fräulein*?' asked Wenzel, surprised. 'There's no running away. There are soldiers everywhere.

'I don't mean us to run away. Could you drive me and my sister a little way towards the battle area? Just to see if . . . just to see if we can get news of Lieutenant von Letzberg?'

The Baroness looked at the white faces of her daughters, and turned away, her eyes bright with unshed tears.

'As you wish, Fräulein,' Wenzel said after a pause. 'But at the first sign of danger, I'll turn us round and be back here before you know it.'

The sky was clouding over now, sporadic cannonade from the lakes and the crackle of isolated musket fire from different directions indicating the French were making good their successes and clearing out the last pockets of resistance.

At the top of a rise, Wenzel halted the carriage and the two women descended to look about them. Everywhere were the marks of carnage, soil trampled and churned by boots and hoofs, trees blasted, farm buildings in ruins. Dead horses lay in grotesque mounds, and retreating infantry, mainly Russin and seemingly oblivious of the carriage and its occupants, hurried past as best they could, given the exhaustion from which the poor wretches suffered and the appalling wounds, at the sight of which Stefanie was forced to look quickly away.

'Who are those?' Magda asked, pointing.

Ahead and below them, less than a mile away, the frozen lakes could be seen clearly. Men were milling about at the edge of them, dragging along the great guns in their midst. Close behind them there was an explosion and a flash of flame. The rear men scattered and, as they watched, the river of small dark figures swelled over onto the ice itself.

'But that is madness!' Stefanie cried. 'They cannot cross the ice. It will not hold.'

'The French are firing on the poor devils,' Wenzel said. 'They've no time to judge the risk. But they won't make it.'

Even as he spoke, one of the guns which the tiny figures had dragged onto the expanse of ice, disappeared abruptly from view, men and horses around it floundering in the freezing water. The mass was thrown into confusion, those in front attempting to turn back, those behind, not realising what was happening, pressing onward. Again the cannon sounded and this time the shot fell ahead of the struggling mass, plunging through the ice on the far side of the lake.

'Are they Austrians?' gasped Magda, horrified.

'No, Fräulein, they are Russians,' Wenzel assured her. 'We must go on, we'll not find the lieutenant here.'

A little further on they had the luck to meet with some retreating Austrian Grenadiers, their once white uniforms now a sad sight. In response to their desperate request for news, they were told that Austrian Hussars, about an hour earlier, had attempted to clear a hamlet held by French sharp shooters, a mile further on. Their informant had seen the Hussars charge.

'They made a brave show—but not many of them came back.'

They hastened on and came upon the hamlet itself. But what a place of desolation, deserted now, except by the dead and dying, no wall left standing in its entirety, doors hanging loose upon their hinges, the air filled with the moans of wounded men.

Stefanie, Wenzel and Magda clambered over the piles of rubbish, between ruined, smoking buildings, calling Andreas frantically by name. Then Stefanie halted at the entry to a narrow alley. An Austrian Hussar lay sprawled on his face beside his dead horse. His head was pillowed on his folded arms so naturally that he looked as though he had lain down there and fallen asleep. Stefanie caught her breath. Forcing back her feelings of fear and of repugnance, she stooped and plucked at the dead man's sleeve, pulling his arm away from his face.

It was not Andreas. Relief, mixed with nausea, surged through her. Her surroundings swayed about her, and she sat down heavily in the mud beside the corpse, unable to move for the moment.

'Fräulein!' Wenzel appeared and pulled her somewhat brusquely to her feet. 'We must go back. There are a lot more fellows coming this way and to my mind, they look like French. We must get back to your gracious lady mother.'

They stumbled back towards the carriage. But as they passed a low wall, a sudden dreadful cry split the air. So despairing, and so filled with agony was it, that it hardly seemed possible that it could have come from a human throat. For a second, Stefanie was stunned and then realised, to her horror, that it came from Magda.

'*Andreas*!' Magda screamed again.

Slumped against a wall, a seated figure with a blood encrusted dolman moved slightly and turned his head to one side.

'*Jeziš-Maria*, it *is* him!' muttered Wenzel, and plunged after Magda who had run, stumbling over the uneven ground, towards the wounded man, and fallen to her knees in the mud beside him, calling his name despairingly.

'Leave him, Fräulein, leave him to me,' Wenzel gasped. 'I'll bring the young gentleman, just you run and open the carriage door.' He stooped and sweeping up the young Hussar into his powerful arms as easily as if he had been a child, he carried him back to the waiting carriage.

'He is dying, he is dying!' wailed Magda, as the carriage lurched homeward. 'There is so much blood. He is dead!'

'No, no, he is unconscious,' Stefanie snapped. 'He has lost so much blood from his wounded arm he has fainted. Pull yourself together, Magda, and give me your scarf. We'll tie his arm to his body to save it being jolted further.'

She bound the scarf as best she could around the injury. Andreas groaned as she touched him, and she bit her lip as her hands came away smeared with blood. The torn sleeve was sodden and embedded in the flesh, and she did not like to think what they would find when they cut the cloth away.

With the unconscious Andreas' head cradled in Magda's arms, they managed to reach home without mishap, but, when they got there, they found the Baroness very alarmed.

'Thank God you are safe! I have been watching

through the spy-glass, and I am sure there are French uniforms coming this way.'

'But what of Andreas? We must hide him!' Magda cried. 'They will kill him!'

'They might take him prisoner,' the Baroness said, passing her hand across her brow. 'And we may suffer too, for sheltering him.'

'You would not refuse to hide him?' Magda whispered.

The Baroness turned on her daughter, and for the first time in her life, Stefanie heard her mother's voice raised in anger to either of them.

'Hold your tongue! I have known that boy since he was a squalling babe in his nurse's arms, and I visited his poor mother at her lying-in! Do you think I have watched him grow up for twenty years, just to surrender him—still little more than a child—to the French? You think I would abandon him *now*?'

'Where can we put him?' Stefanie asked, in the ensuing silence.

'In the cellar,' the Baroness spoke in a sharp practical voice, her calm restored. 'We shall have to hide him down there till tonight. Wenzel, carry the lieutenant. Janko will help you. Hanka, bring blankets. We must wrap him warmly. The cellar is cold.'

They carried Andreas down into the dark, icy cellar and made him as comfortable as was possible, contriving to conceal him behind the stack of firewood and the various barrels and boxes.

'I wish we could look at that wound now,' the Baroness fretted. 'But it must wait. Girls, you must go upstairs and change your gowns, those are stained with blood. Burn the stained ones. Hurry! If the French see traces of blood, they will know we have a wounded man here.'

Stefanie and Magda ran upstairs, struggling out of their blood-soaked dresses and into clean ones. Hanka seized the soiled gowns and pushed them onto the kitchen fire, where they smouldered, filling the kitchen with foul smelling smoke.

They had barely time to dispose of the last traces and to wash their hands clean, before Janko's voice was heard calling loudly: 'Ladies, ladies! There are two French Dragoons before the door!'

CHAPTER
ELEVEN

THE two Dragoons dismounted in the evening gloom and came into the house. One had lost his helmet, and his face was a ghastly red mask, covered in blood stemming from a long open gash which laid bare his face from ear to chin. The other Dragoon, splashed from head to toe with mud, but apparently uninjured, removed his leopard skin bound helmet as he entered, stamping his boots to shake off some of the thickly caked mud.

'Why, Monsieur de Vaudry . . . ' the Baroness faltered.

'So we have all survived,' he said brusquely, his glance sweeping the room and taking in Stefanie and Magda. He did not greet either of them. 'I present to you a comrade-in-arms,' he indicated the Red Mask. 'Sit down, Lucien, and try not to drip on madame's carpet.'

'Your servant, Ladies,' said Red Mask faintly, and collapsed onto a chair.

'You have needle and thread?' Léon demanded of the Baroness.

'Why, yes—'

'Bring it, quickly!' He gestured impatiently with his hand.

The Baroness hunted in a sewing box and produced the required articles. 'I am sure, monsieur, if you have some damage to your uniform, we should be happy—'

'Give it to me. Uniform repairs you can do later, if you want. I want to sew up poor Lucien's face here. As you can see, a Russian did his best to decapitate him.' He held out his hand for the needle.

'Sew—! But, monsieur, should not a doctor attend your friend?'

'I dare say I can do as good a job as an army surgeon in this case. Quicker, too. The field hospital is full. Hold up, Lucien, *mon vieux*. By the time I've finished with you, you'll have a scar that will be the talk of Paris. You'll be surrounded by young ladies on your return, all hanging on your arm and wanting to know your daring exploits.'

'Shut up and get on with it,' muttered the patient ungratefully. 'By the time *you* finish, I shall wish the Russian had taken better aim!'

The Captain proceeded to accomplish his task, stitching up the wound neatly and rapidly. Apart from a sharp grunt when the needle first penetrated the skin, the wounded Dragoon sat perfectly still, giving every appearance of unconcern.

'I don't believe they are human,' Magda whispered in awe.

'I'll fetch some brandy for your patient, monsieur,' said the Baroness in a faint voice, looking as if she might need some of this stimulant herself.

'Obliged to you,' muttered the wounded man. He got to his feet and lurched to the mirror, peering at the Captain's handiwork.

'Come along, we've no time for you to admire yourself,' Léon told him unkindly. 'Drink madame la baronne's brandy and be off.' He turned to the women. 'I'll come back later, and sleep here tonight. I want a bath. You can start heating water now, so it will be ready by the time I return.'

He nodded at them and, propelling his comrade by the elbow ahead of him, strode out, the door clashing to behind them.

Stefanie stood, rooted to the spot. Was this the man

who had written such a love letter to her as she had read earlier? So sincere, so devoted . . . He had not even greeted her! Had not addressed her one word! He had only entered, demanded what he wanted, and gone. Later he would be back, once again demanding their hospitality, shelter and care. Was this what victory did to a man? She remembered him coming into the room on the day the jubilant French had entered Vienna. He had been so confident, so arrogant, had assumed such rights. Now she saw him like that again.

'He wrote that letter because he believed he was going to die!' she thought angrily. 'But now he is very much alive—and tomorrow is another day!'

The letter. He would demand the return of his letter when he came back and would see the broken seal and know she had read it!

'But what are we to do with Andreas now?' Magda cried in despair. 'If the Captain is in the house, how can we hide him?'

'We might throw ourselves and Andreas on the Captain's mercy,' the Baroness suggested doubtfully.

'No!' Stefanie replied vigorously. 'We cannot trust him! Vienna was an open city, and the French were on their best behaviour there. But now everything is changed. He is the victor: we are the vanquished. Whatever he was before, that is *all* he is now!'

'We cannot leave Andreas in the cellar, he will catch pneumonia,' Magda protested. 'Or bleed to death.'

'He will have to stay in the cellar until after the Captain is asleep tonight. Then we'll smuggle him upstairs somehow. We'll go down now, and see how he is.'

Lantern in hand, and accompanied by Wenzel, the girls descended the cellar steps and made their way to the corner where they had concealed the wounded Andreas. They could hear him muttering feverishly to himself in delirium.

'I hope he isn't going to start shouting out when

Léon—the Captain—gets back,' Stefanie said worriedly. She lifted the lantern and gave a cry. Two wicked little red eyes stared at her in the sudden light. A huge rat, attracted by the smell of blood, was crouched on the helpless man's chest. Twitching its whiskers and long scaly tail, it sat up and stared at them boldly, as if it would dispute its find with them.

Wenzel swore and threw a piece of firewood at the creature. It leapt off the wounded man and dashed, not away, but towards them. They could see its razor-sharp white teeth. Wenzel lifted his foot and stamped heavily on the rat's head, crushing it.

'Has it bitten him?' Stefanie knelt over Andreas and searched for the dreaded teeth marks. 'No, I think not.' She heaved a sigh of relief. 'But we were only just in time. Wenzel, we cannot leave him here.'

'Someone must stay with him, Ladies, and keep the vermin off. The rats know he's here, and they'll be back.'

'I'll stay,' Magda said firmly.

'No, Magda, you are afraid of the rats,' Stefanie protested.

'Yes, I am,' Magda said in a quiet, cold little voice. 'But I'll pick them up with my bare hands if they attack Andreas.'

'That doesn't sound a good idea, little lady,' said Wenzel gently, 'I'll stay with the poor young man. Anyway, you must all be there when the Frenchman returns, or he'll miss you, and want to know where you are.'

'I hope the Captain doesn't come late,' Magda fretted as they returned upstairs. 'Or it will be hours before we get Andreas out of that dreadful cellar.'

Stefanie was worried too, and wondered whether, after all, it might not be better to appeal to Léon when he came. But that all rather depended on what mood he was in.

Before he came, however, they were to receive other visitors. Janko was hauling up buckets of water from the well, and Hanka boiling it on the fire for the bath. Magda and her mother were hastily preparing a bedroom for the Captain, and Stefanie had cut up some bread and sausage and put it on a tray with some wine. She carried it into the sitting room and had just set it down on a table, when there was a sudden crash from the hall, and a strange man's voice called out in French. The door swung open, and two French infantrymen burst into the room.

When they saw her, they stopped and stared. Their uniforms were stained and torn, and their faces unshaven and dirty, but their manner, once they had recovered from their momentary surprise, was bold and truculent. Men such as these had supplied the mobs which had run beside the tumbrils, twelve years earlier in France, and Stefanie was in no illusion as regarded her own safety.

'What do you want?' she demanded of them sternly, although her heart was in her mouth. She suspected they might be of peasant origin, and instinct told her the only hope was to dominate them by sheer force of character, trusting that the respect born of centuries of subservience to the seigneur in his château, would not be quite dead in these two. But if they proved the spawn of the gutters of Paris, or the harbour of Marseilles, there was nothing she could do.

Her manner did impress them briefly and made them hesitate. Then the nearer of the two grinned, showing broken, yellow teeth.

'Well, we're in fine company,' he said, moving into the room, and looking covetously about him. 'Fine house, fine things . . .' He took hold of one of the velvet drapes and jerked viciously at it. It broke loose and tumbled down into his arms.

'How dare you? Just where do you think you are?

Who gave you permission to enter here?' she cried angrily.

He brandished the musket he held. 'Here's my pass, mam'zelle! This lets me enter, even here!'

'Now, what do you think of mademoiselle here?' The other soldier, tall, lanky, with wolfish, deep-set eyes, spoke for the first time, though he had been staring at her since he had come in. 'Isn't she a pretty one?' He reached out a hand as hairy and yellow-nailed as a wolf's paw, and touched her blonde hair lecherously.

'Don't you dare to lay a hand on me!' She struck the odious hand away, trying to keep the fear from her voice. *Never let them see it* . . . the doomed comte de Vaudry had warned his son.

The soldier drew in a sharp breath, and was about to reach out to seize hold of her, when, from the doorway, came the unmistakable rasp of cold steel.

The two men heard it and froze, the one with his hand still stretched out towards Stefanie. Then they both turned slowly towards the door, and the fearsome sight of Léon, who stood menacingly in the doorway, drawn sabre in hand, blocking their escape. The look in his eyes would have struck terror in the most foolhardy soul.

The soldier with the velvet drape in his arms quickly threw his booty to the floor, and whined ingratiatingly, 'We mean to make no trouble, Captain, just looking around . . .'

As he spoke, the other soldier backed slowly towards the nearest window which had not yet been shuttered. Suddenly he turned and made a dash, wrenching open the catch of the inner window. With the most blood-curdling yell Stefanie had ever heard, Léon leapt forward, the gleaming blade of the sabre flashing as he whirled the murderous weapon above his head. And execution was quite evidently his intention, for the razor-like blade would have sliced the man's head from his shoulders, had it made contact. With screams of fear, the soldier, having no time to open the outer of the double windows, hurled himself head-first through it, to effect his escape, in a welter of crashing, shattered glass. His companion scooped up the fallen drape, and hurled it into Léon's face, deflecting the fatal blow. Then he leapt after his fellow, and they landed outside, entangled with one another. They scrambled madly to their feet, and ran off as fast as they could go, blood streaming from the cuts they had sustained in their flight, and leaving their muskets behind them.

The Baroness had come running into the room, and now stood, white-faced, with her arm about Stefanie's shoulders. 'We are again in your debt, monsieur,' she said to Léon with some difficulty.

Léon, panting heavily, turned from the window, putting up the sabre. In a cold voice he said abruptly, 'I apologise for your being disturbed in such a way. It is not our policy to harass civilians. We seek only to round up escaping Russian and Austrian soldiers.'

Stefanie exchanged a quick warning glance with Magda. Inwardly she was thinking, 'He would have struck down two of their own men without a moment's hesitation!' and this glimpse of the brutal, on the spot justice sometimes meted out in the Grand Army, filled her with a horror which transcended any fear she had felt for herself, and made her more determined than ever not to place Andreas at the Captain's mercy.

'You would no doubt like something to eat, monsieur,' the Baroness said quickly, indicating the tray. 'We have put a supper for you. Only bread and sausage, I am afraid. It is all we have.'

'No matter,' he answered, as if he really did not care much. Without warning, he put his hand against the wall and staggered slightly.

Stefanie instinctively started forward, despite all her thoughts, exclaiming, 'You are injured!'

'No, no, I'm all right. Not even a scratch,' he muttered, putting out a hand to ward her off.

The Baroness went up to him and took his arm. 'Come, Monsieur de Vaudry, come and sit down. Stefanie, take the Captain's other arm.'

It was exhaustion, purely and simply. He was tired out. He sat down heavily on the sofa, his face grey beneath the tan and the mud, and smiled crookedly up at the Baroness.

'Your supper will be my breakfast, madame. I'll eat it tomorrow.' He leaned back and closed his eyes.

The Baroness shook him forcibly by the shoulder. 'Don't go to sleep there, Captain! Your bath is ready. Go and take that, and sleep in a proper bed.'

'Yes, yes . . .' he mumbled, and wandered out of the door in a disorientated manner.

'I don't think we need fear he will hear us move Andreas,' the Baroness whispered. 'He'll sleep so soundly, the trumpets of Judgment would not wake him. But we've put him in the room furthest from the staircase, just to make sure.'

'I'm really worried about Andreas,' Stefanie said in a low voice to her mother. 'There is something dreadfully wrong with that arm, and we won't be able to set it like a simple broken bone.'

'We'll see. If matters are really as bad as you fear, we shall have no choice but to throw ourselves on the clemency of Monsieur de Vaudry tomorrow.'

'No, I won't let you!' cried Magda, overhearing. 'You heard what he said. They are hunting down our soldiers. He'll take Andreas prisoner, he'll take him away! I won't let anyone take him away from me.'

'Hush, child, we are all tired, and tomorrow things may not look so bleak.'

'I'll go and see what's happening to our French guest,' Stefanie said. 'I want to move Andreas as soon as possible.'

She went out of the room and listened. The house seemed quite quiet and she could hear no one moving about upstairs. 'Hanka will know,' she thought, making her way towards the kitchen.

As she approached the kitchen door, she heard the cook's voice. It was exclaiming something loudly, and sounded, unbelievably, almost jolly. Curious, Stefanie pushed open the kitchen door quietly, and peeped in.

Steam filled the room. The fire had been built up with logs and roared up into the chimney. Before it, in a large wooden wash-tub banded with iron, sat the Captain, stark naked, and conducting a lively and hilarious conversation of the most doubtful respectability with Hanka, in an extraordinary mixture of French, German and what sounded like Polish. Hanka, convulsed with laughter, was scrubbing his back energetically. Her chins wobbled and the tears ran down her face. The Captain, tough, resilient, and as unpredictable as ever, had apparently made a temporary recovery from his exhaustion, and was, as ever, making himself at home.

Red with embarrassment and fury, Stefanie closed the door quickly and quietly, before they saw her, and crept away.

'He's taking his bath,' she said woodenly to her mother and Magda. 'And I think he's feeling better.'

Their fears that the Captain's apparent recovery might lead to his re-appearance were unfounded, however. Hanka came shortly afterwards to report that the French officer had gone to bed, laconically declaring to the cook that he was '*kaput*' as he went.

'He's a one, that Frenchman,' said Hanka. 'The things he was saying! It made my sides ache, I laughed that much.'

'How could you joke with him, Hanka?' Stefanie accused her angrily. 'With poor Lieutenant von Letzberg lying in the cellar?'

'Bless you, my dear little lady, I haven't forgotten the

poor Austrian boy. Janko and Václav are bringing him upstairs now.'

'They must take care!' the Baroness exclaimed, hastening out of the room.

'But perhaps the Captain isn't asleep yet,' Magda protested. 'Suppose we get half way up the stairs and he suddenly appears? You know what he's like. He says he's tired out, but one can't be sure. He's the most unpredictable man.'

'Go with Mama, I'll go and listen at his door,' Stefanie pushed her sister after their mother. Then she ran upstairs and put her ear to the door panels of the Captain's room. She thought she could detect heavy, regular breathing, but was not sure. Candle in hand, she turned the handle cautiously, and entered.

A trail of clothing started by the door and stretched across the floor to the bed, indicating the Captain had progressed erratically to his rest, shedding garments as he went. His boots had been tossed into the corner of the room, and his sword belt hung on the bedpost. Léon himself was sound asleep in the middle of the bed.

Stefanie stooped to pick up his coat and hang it on a chairback, before tip-toeing across the room to hold the candle above his recumbent form. The feather pillows had been pushed together in a heap, and the Captain's head was buried in them, face down, so that all she could see was his curly black hair. She wondered he could breathe at all, and had a nightmare vision of his suffocating during the night, and their having to explain his demise to the French Command in the morning. Tentatively, she moved the topmost pillow slightly, to give him more air. To her alarm, he threw himself over onto his back, trapping her hand beneath his naked shoulder.

'Oh, no!' Stefanie thought, trying to ease her hand out from beneath him. She had just managed to free it when, without warning, he opened his eyes, and stared straight up at her.

He was probably still more than half asleep, for he frowned in a puzzled way, screwing up his face like a child which has been wakened, and muttered vaguely, 'Stefanie?'

'Shh!' she whispered hastily, shielding the flame of the candle with her hand.

'You . . .' he murmured, throwing his arm out towards her.

'No, no . . . go back to sleep!' she said soothingly.

He blinked two or three times, grimacing up at the candlelight and she began to back cautiously away.

Suddenly his voice came clearly. 'Wait!' The hand he had flung out towards her seized her skirt and held her fast.

Stefanie bit her lip to stop a cry of despair and alarm. The candle tilted, spilling hot wax onto her wrist, and she set it down hastily onto the bedside table, and tried to prise her skirt free from his grasp. But in releasing the material, he caught at her fingers instead.

'Don't run away,' he said quietly. He pushed himself up on one elbow and grinned crookedly at her.

She was trapped here within the glow of candlelight —as she had been trapped with him in the dining room in Vienna, it seemed an age ago, and she glimpsed that same look again in his eyes she remembered so well from that fateful evening.

'Léon . . .' she whispered. 'Let me go, I can't stay. I must go.'

'Then why did you come?' he asked simply.

'I . . .' What could she say? How else could it seem to him other than that she had come to him at last. What possible alternative explanation could she put forward which he would accept? 'I wanted to see if you were all right,' she offered feebly.

'All the better were you here with me, *ma belle*!' he said invitingly and, seeing her look of alarm, whispered coaxingly, 'Come on, don't look so frightened . . . it won't be martyrdom. I promise!'

'You don't understand! I can't stay . . . Oh, Léon, please let me go!'

She tried to pull her hand free, but he gave a mischievous chuckle and flinging his other arm round her, dragged her down onto the bed beside him. The feather pillow sank beneath their combined weight and they descended into a warm nest moulding itself to the contours of their bodies, whilst the wooden bedstead creaked protestingly.

Stefanie, her alarm reinforced by the fear that the Baroness might come in to see what took her so long, pushed desperately at his bare chest as he tried to kiss her, feeling the throb of his heart against the palm of her hand.

'Léon, stop! You *must* listen to me!'

'Mmn . . .? I'm listening . . .' he murmured, nuzzling her neck.

'No, you're not! Léon, stop it!'

He gave a sigh. 'All right. What is it now?'

As Stefanie opened her mouth to speak, she heard a faint distant clatter from the floor below. Wenzel and Janko had brought the wounded Andreas up from the cellar. Fearing Léon might also notice the movement in the house, she began to whisper quickly and urgently. 'My mother knows I came to see if you were all right. If I don't go back soon . . .'

'She'll understand where you are,' he said calmly. 'She won't come in.' He ran his fingers over her corn-gold hair, spread across the pillow like a silken net.

Stefanie looked up into his face, so close to hers in the yellow candlelight. 'Léon . . .' she said hesitantly. 'It's not that I don't understand . . .' She began to feel wretched, thinking of the hideous scenes he must have witnessed that day, of close friends dead, perhaps, possibly a brush with Death himself. To refuse him comfort now seemed in itself a dreadful thing. 'I can't, Léon,' she said dully. 'I can't do as you want . . . not now, not—'

He made no reply, and did not move, making no attempt to stop her and she slipped out from his encircling arm. Standing by the bedside, she pushed back her dishevelled hair and took up the candle.

Léon sat up, resting his arms on his bent knees, and laced his fingers together. He stared at her thoughtfully. 'Go on,' he said.

'There's nothing more to be said, not now. You're tired, you should sleep—this has been a dreadful day. We'll talk about it all tomorrow. Please . . .'

For what seemed a very long time he did not speak, but sat studying her face, thrown into relief by the flickering flame of the candle she held. The glow struck her cheekbones, highlighting them, and casting shadows into the hollows in which her eyes seemed to burn luminously. His own face was in semi-darkness now and the features only dimly discernible. She could not see how he looked, and was glad of it, knowing that it would take only a very little to destroy her resolution.

'*Va-t'en, alors,*' he said eventually in a flat, expressionless voice. 'Go along, then.'

With a sudden, brusque movement, he threw himself down and rolled over away from her, burying his face in the pillows as it had been before. She waited for a few minutes, but he did not stir. Over the years he had learned to snatch at slumber at will, under the menacing shadow of the Committee of Public Safety, against the thunder of the guns, with throbbing wounds and the pangs of hunger and thirst, even on horseback. And he slept now, blotting out another pain, one she had inflicted.

With an echoing ache in her own heart, Stefanie went outside and softly closed the door.

'It's all right,' she told the others, who waited at the

foot of the stairs. 'He won't disturb us.'

'Where shall we put the young gentleman?' whispered Janko.

'Put him in my room,' Stefanie said. 'It's the nearest, and the furthest from the Captain.'

They carried Andreas into the room and put him on the bed. He was conscious now, but his eyes were bright with fever. With scissors, the Baroness carefully cut away the sleeve on which the blood had dried, and, taking a deep breath, eased the material away from the wound.

'It's terrible!' whispered Magda. 'It's . . .'

Janko gulped and turned aside abruptly, mopping his brow. *'Jeziš-Maria,'* he muttered.

'Grape-shot,' Wenzel opined. 'I reckon. Nearly took the arm off, smashed it completely. What shall we do, *gnä' Frau*?'

'Bind it up for now, we can do nothing else. In the morning, we'll look at it again, in daylight.'

They divided the night into three watches, to sit by the wounded Hussar. The Baroness took the first, Magda was to take the second, and Stefanie the dawn watch. She went to Magda's room and lay down upon the bed, resting her hand on her forehead. For an hour or two they had respite. But in the morning Léon would awake, refreshed, and keenly observant. How long could they hope to keep the secret of Andreas' presence then?

CHAPTER
TWELVE

Dawn broke greyly, and Stefanie, rising from the bedside of the wounded Andreas, drew back the curtains
and opened the shutters. Woodsmoke hung in the air
from the fires of the victorious French army camped all
around them. She returned to the bed and bent over
Andreas. All night he had tossed, muttering and mumb-
ling to himself. Now he opened his eyes and fixed his
gaze on her.

'Andreas? Do you know me?' she asked gently.

He tried to speak, but was unable and only nodded
weakly. Quickly she poured out some water and held it
to his lips.

'Magda . . .' he muttered.

'She'll come soon. Just rest.'

He tried to move and groaned. 'My arm . . .'

Stefanie turned back the sheet and tried to keep her
face impassive as she inspected the wound, not wishing
Andreas to see her anxiety. As she bent over it, a curious
sweet odour rose to strike her nostrils from the clotted
bandages. It reminded her of something . . . of a brace
of well hung pheasant. She swallowed hard and put back
the coverlet.

'I . . . cannot . . . stay here . . .' Andreas whispered.
He reached out his sound arm and clutched feebly at her
hand. 'The French . . .'

'Hush, lie still. No one knows you are here.' She
hesitated. 'But, Andreas, you must not make any noise.
You must not cry out, although I know you are in pain.
There is a French officer sleeping in the house. There is

no reason why he should find you, but you *must* be quiet. Do you understand?'

He nodded.

A little later the door opened to admit Magda. She, too, looked up white-faced from the wounded arm, her eyes, dilated with fear, fixed on her sister.

'Wenzel will have to ride to Brünn for a doctor,' Stefanie whispered.

'But how should we explain a doctor coming here?' Magda asked.

'We shall say, one of us is sick.' Stefanie twisted her hands nervously. 'You were ill the evening before we left Vienna, and Léon knows it. If we say you have been taken ill again, he will accept it.'

'Mama has spoken to Wenzel already,' Magda returned disconsolately. 'Wenzel says he will try, but is afraid no doctor will come, because of the French.'

'I'll go and speak to Wenzel. Stay here, Magda.' Stefanie went out of the room quietly and closed the door.

Outside, she leaned against the wall and closed her eyes briefly, before wiping the cold perspiration from her brow. Nausea rose and fell in her, all the reaction from the smell of the wound which she had forced down earlier. She quite failed to hear the approach of anyone else, until a concerned voice said, 'You are not well!' and a hand touched her arm.

Léon stood beside her. He was in his shirt-sleeves, and had apparently just come upstairs.

She stared at him in unconcealed dismay. 'What are *you* doing here?' she gasped.

'Nothing—I've just been downstairs and given my coat to your cook to be mended. Stefanie, what's wrong? You look like Death. Here, is this your room? Let me help you inside—'

'No, no!' She pushed his helping hand away. 'I'm all right!'

'You don't look it, my sweet. Come on, you must go and lie down.' He reached out his hand for the door handle.

'No, you must not!' She grasped his wrist in an agony.

'Look,' he said patiently, 'I'm not trying to gain admittance to your room for the purpose of seducing you—I just want you to go and lie down, before you fall down at my feet!'

'But I'm not ill, I—'

In vain, she attempted to prevent him. He had turned the handle and pushed opened the door. It swung open wide, revealing the whole sight of the bed, its wounded occupant and Magda.

Seeing the Frenchman, Magda let out a piercing shriek and threw herself in front of Andreas, who began to struggle weakly, trying to drag himself upright on the pillows.

Leon released the door handle and walked slowly into the room. He looked first at Magda's terrified face, and then at the wounded man.

'I see,' he said expressionlessly, though a hard note had entered his voice. 'Allow me to hazard a guess. Would I be correct in assuming this to be young von Letzberg?'

'Yes . . .' Stefanie admitted.

'You shall not touch him! You shan't come near him!' Magda screamed at Léon wildly, throwing out her arms and placing herself squarely between him and the bed.

'Léon . . .' Stefanie faltered, but fell silent at the look he gave her.

He began to move slowly and deliberately towards the bed, and Magda, remarking calmly, 'Well, boy, let's have a look at you.'

'No!' Magda barred the way desperately.

'Léon!' Stefanie cried pleadingly. 'Don't you see he is wounded and defenceless?'

'Oh yes, I can see that!' he flung harshly at her. 'Get

your sister out of the way. I only want to look at his injuries. I don't intend to finish him off!' he added sarcastically.

'You will have to kill me first, before I let you touch him!' Magda cried vibrantly. 'I swear it!'

'Come, little Magda,' he said very quietly and gently. 'You know *me*. You don't think I would harm your lover? It is *Léon*—Léon, for whose waltz lessons you played the piano in Vienna. Do you not trust me?'

Indecision crossed Magda's face. 'You will take him away. He will die!'

'I will not hurt him, I swear. Come now, I know more of battle wounds than you. Let me take a look . . .' He continued to speak reasonably and persuasively. 'You are not afraid of me, Magda?'

Tears filled Magda's eyes, but she moved slowly and unwillingly aside.

'That's better. All right, my young friend,' he put a hand on Andreas' shoulder and pushed him gently but firmly back onto the pillows. 'There's no need for alarm. Just let me see the damage.'

He inspected the wounded arm closely, and then gave a grunt. Coming back across the room, he took Stefanie's elbow, and bundled her roughly out into the corridor.

'Now!' he said as the door closed on them, and speaking in that low, hard voice which always terrified her so. 'Now, mademoiselle, perhaps you'd be so good as to explain to me what the devil you think you're playing at! How long has he been here?' His eyes flashed angrily at her.

'We found him yesterday—before you came. We hid him in the cellar, and brought him upstairs when you were asleep,' she confessed, petrified.

'You mean to tell me, you left that boy *down in a cellar* all yesterday evening? Why? *Why*?' he demanded harshly.

'We were afraid you—' her voice faded and choked.

'You were afraid I would what? Well, what did you imagine I would do? Murder him, perhaps?'

'No, no, of course not! But you must see—'

'I see you were afraid of me, and thought *I* would harm him! You, Stefanie, *you*, of all people, could not trust me that much?'

'I . . .'

'So, you think I make war on wounded men, do you?' he went on, and when she did not reply, he grasped her arm roughly and shook it so violently that she cried out in pain. 'Answer me, damn you! Is that what you think?'

'No, Léon, no! Only, we thought you might take him prisoner.'

'Prisoner? We have thousands of prisoners! What should I want with another wounded junior lieutenant? Especially one who will never ride out to fight again.'

'What do you mean?' she whispered.

He released her. 'The arm is mortifying . . . gangrene will set in. Could you not smell it? I have smelled that stench too often not to know what it means.' He took a deep breath. 'I promised Magda I would not hurt him —but if his life is to be saved, the arm must come off, and as soon as possible.'

'Amputated? But we cannot—' she stared at him in horror.

'No, *we* cannot. I'll go now and try to persuade one of our army surgeons to come. They are busy enough, God knows, with our men, but one or two of them are not bad fellows, and might come to look at an Austrian. Keep young von Letzberg quiet. Don't say anything of it to him until I return.'

'Where has he gone?' demanded Magda tremulously. 'He has gone to fetch soldiers!'

'No, no', Stefanie assured her. 'He has gone to fetch help.' She went to watch from the window. 'He would not lie to me . . .' she thought. 'He would not send men to take Andreas prisoner.'

It was an hour and a half before she saw two horsemen ride up to the house and ran down to meet them. It was Léon, accompanied by an unshaven young man in muddy top boots and a creased blue coat.

'The surgeon . . .' Léon said briefly, indicating this unpromising looking individual.

'We are obliged to you, monsieur,' Stefanie said uncertainly, if anything more alarmed by the sight of such a disreputable looking person, than she would have been at the sight of a party of armed men.

'Well, where is he?' demanded the surgeon ungraciously. 'I've been up all night, cutting up good Frenchman, and if I'm to start on the Austrian army, too, I can't afford to waste time!'

'Don't be put off by his manner. They are not supposed to treat the enemy, unless it's a general's life at stake! He takes a risk in coming here. No one must know,' Léon whispered to her as they followed the surgeon upstairs. 'I know this one well. He is a decent fellow, and only a surgeon to the army because of gaming debts at home—unlike most of his colleagues, who hold their posts because of incompetence!'

They led the surgeon to the injured man's bedside, where he took off his coat, revealing shirt linen smeared with brown stains which hardly inspired more confidence than his rakish appearance. He examined the wound briefly, then straightened up, so that his eye fell on Magda, whose pretty face was distorted by terror.

'Madame,' said the surgeon to the Baroness, 'you'll oblige me by taking that little one out of here. I can't be distracted by hysterical women.'

Speaking soothingly to her daughter, the Baroness managed, with difficulty, to lead Magda away, leaving Stefanie and Léon in the room.

'You'll have to lose the arm, my friend,' said the

surgeon to Andreas. 'Do you understand what I say?'

'Yes,' Andreas whispered in French. 'I understand you.'

The surgeon stared at him briefly, and then patted him not unkindly on the shoulder. 'Don't worry, it won't take me long.' He turned to Léon and Stefanie. 'Mademoiselle, your cook has not a well-sharpened knife, by any chance? Mine have become blunted through much use these last few hours. And if you have any brandy, you had better bring it.'

Stefanie went downstairs and fetched the knife, washing it carefully.

'Hold the blade into the flames for a second or two,' Janko advised. He took it from her and passed the glinting blade above the kitchen fire, whistling sharply to himself as he nearly burned his fingers. 'Here,' he said, returning it to her. 'It will be cooled down by the time you get upstairs. My old grandad always used to do that. He was a farrier. He reckoned, if he had to open up a cyst, or something like that on a horse, the knife did a better job, if you did that first . . .'

When she came back, both Léon and the surgeon were in rolled up shirt-sleeves, and the surgeon was searching in his bag.

'I have no laudanum left, so you will have to hold the patient down, Captain,' he said in a low voice to Léon. He glanced at Stefanie. 'Do you feel yourself able to assist me, mademoiselle?'

'Yes,' Stefanie said firmly, though her stomach heaved at the thought.

'I doubt you have ever seen your cook wring a chicken's neck,' said Léon unsympathetically. 'If you can't do it, go and fetch someone who can. Don't play at being brave.'

'I will do it!' she flared at him.

'Then cover up that pretty gown,' said the surgeon in a practical voice. 'And you are *not* to faint, do you hear me? No one will have time for you, if you do, and you will be left lying on the floor, where you will be in the way!'

He bent over Andreas and the blade slit into the skin, lifting it just below the shoulder. Andreas jerked convulsively as Léon threw all his weight across him, and the surgeon growled, 'Hold him *down*!' Though badly shaken, Stefanie found she had no time to faint, as the blade continued to cut through the mangled flesh and sinew, the surgeon's aim being to take the arm off at the shoulder joint. Léon had chosen his man well. The surgeon, for all his youth and neglected appearance, was certainly competent, and a believer in the necessity for speed. Only once did he speak, and that was in mid-operation, to exclaim sharply, 'Hold up, he is going! The brandy!'

Léon forced the brandy between the patient's lips, and then it was finished, and the surgeon was rinsing his hands in the bowl on the bedside cabinet, the water gradually turning a bright reddish orange. Andreas lay on the bloodstained pillows, grey-faced, and groaning with pain.

'Well, mademoiselle, it is up to you now,' the surgeon said. He dried his hands wearily on the towel she handed him, his tiredness showing in his face. 'I shall not be able to come back. Others need me.'

'Yes, monsieur, we understand,' she said soberly.

She led the surgeon downstairs, where Hanka wept into her apron, and stood before the house in the chill wind whilst he mounted his horse and gathered up the reins.

'We are deeply grateful to you, monsieur,' Stefanie said, laying a hand on the horse's neck. 'We realise that there are some who would not be pleased to think you had come here.'

The young man looked down at her earnest face, and a dry smile touched the corners of his mouth. 'I assure you, mademoiselle, we surgeons are a despised race, and accustomed to censure. Since no one likes us anyway, it makes little difference whether anyone approves of our actions! I came here to oblige de Vaudry. He—er—is a notable cardplayer! I have owed him too much money in the past to be able to refuse a request from him now.' He smiled at her openly.

'I do not believe that is the reason you came,' she told him. 'And you know that we, at least, do not despise you. Yours is an unenviable and thankless task, monsieur.'

'Yes,' he said, 'and if you could see how some army surgeons perform their duties, you would understand why the soldier fears and reviles us. But some of us, at least, try to do the best we can . . . in the circumstances.'

'Your efforts will win recognition, I am sure,' Stefanie insisted.

'Perhaps,' he said, settling his feet in the stirrups. Suddenly he burst out, 'Do you know what I would do? I would gather up the Imperial standards, flags, eagles, everything, and dispose of them somewhere in the deepest part of the ocean, whence they could never be recovered! In a field hospital, mademoiselle, there is where you learn the true price of Glory!' He touched his hat and rode quickly away.

Stefanie walked slowly indoors. The ribbon which bound back her hair had slipped, and she put up a hand absently to pull it loose, so that her hair fell forward freely round her face. Twisting the ribbon in her fingers, she climbed the stairs thoughtfully.

Léon leaned against the doorframe of the bedroom, watching Magda, who sat beside Andreas, bathing his forehead and murmuring consolation and endearments. There was something in the Dragoon's dark eyes which wrenched at Stefanie's heart, it was so lost-looking and despairing. But when he saw her, he pulled himself together and whispered, 'This is no place for us—come,' and he took her hand and led her back to the sitting room.

There, released from unnatural restraints and unable to prevent herself, Stefanie burst into tears of grief and shock.

'Come along,' he said gently, putting his arm around her and squeezing her shaking shoulders comfortingly, 'it is over. You have been so brave, don't give way now.'

'It is Andreas,' sobbed Stefanie. 'He suffered so much and did not even cry out. He is only a boy—'

'No, he is a man!' he said sharply. 'He'll live. He has someone to live for—' He fell silent and took his arm from her shoulders. When she had controlled her tears, he went on seriously, 'Stefanie, all this has perhaps served a purpose. It has at least shown me what you really feel, about me. I wrote you a letter. It was a mistake. I should not have done so. I would like to have it back.'

'I'm *sorry*, Léon!' she said wildly. 'It wasn't that I mistrusted you—'

'Didn't you? Is that why that young Hussar was left for hours in a cellar where he might have bled to death?'

Silenced, Stefanie took the letter from her pocket and handed it to him.

He turned it over, his dark gaze resting on the broken seal. Looking up, into her eyes, he said enigmatically, 'You read it, then?'

'Yes,' Stefanie answered, barely audibly.

'Think a cannonball had taken my head off, did you? Or just curious?' he asked in his old, cynical way.

'*Don't*, Léon!' she burst out. 'Don't! You hurt me, and you hurt yourself!'

'Yes,' he said. 'Yes, I do.'

'Surely you cannot believe it was curiosity?' she cried, adding miserably, 'I wanted to be with you—and I was with you, when I read your letter.'

'*You* are always with me,' he said with quiet sincerity.

'Even in battle?'

'Even there.'

'And yet you did not even greet me, when you came with your fellow Dragoon.'

'I came as quickly as I could yesterday, partly because it was the nearest source of help for poor Lucien, it is true. But mostly because I was afraid some ill might have befallen you all. When I saw you were all safe, then my concern was for Lucien's wound. I apologise if my manners were at fault, *chére mademoiselle*, and not suitable for a Viennese drawing room! Perhaps you would like to consider where and what I had come from!'

'Yes, of course. I was stupid, I don't know what I expected,' Stefanie paused. 'How was poor Monsieur Lucien when you left him? Will his face heal?'

'He was well enough, and writing letters to his sweetheart, promising to come home in the Spring and marry her—if she doesn't mind the look of him.'

'She won't mind a scar or two, not if she loves him. She will only be glad to have him return.'

'Women are strange creatures,' he said. 'Perhaps she'll be pleased to see him, and perhaps she won't. There are plenty of handsome young officers with their faces all in one piece.'

'That's a cruel thing to say!' she cried accusingly.

'I've seen it happen . . . Women may be God's loveliest creations, but what makes you think they are never cruel? The more beautiful, the more cruel. I've known men who have looked Death in the face a dozen times without flinching, destroyed in a minute by a single sentence from a woman. It is more easily done that you suppose . . .' his voice faltered slightly. Then he went on, 'Few have a heart as true and courageous as Magda's. Perhaps Lucien's sweetheart is just a pretty, silly little miss with no malice in her heart at all, but who will not be able to hide the fact that his appearance repells her . . . that she cannot bear him to touch her. I once saw a man, no older than Lucien, not yet five and twenty, ride out deliberately under the great guns for no better reason.'

'Do you think I would not love you, Léon,' she asked soberly, 'if you were maimed like Andreas, or disfigured, like Lucien?'

'Would you? I don't even know you love me now.' He gave her a look which was both sad and tired, yet questing.

'Yes, you do!' Stefanie told him passionately. 'You know it very well. How can you say you do not know I love you, when you must know it every time you put your arms around me or kiss me? You do not have to torment me like this to force me to say it!'

'I torment you?' he flung at her. 'I would die for you! It is you who torment me. You have no faith in me, no trust in me, nothing! Even having read this,' he brandished the letter in her face, 'even then, you could not believe in me!'

When she did not reply, he turned on his heel and strode to the door, disappearing towards the kitchen. A moment or two later, he was back, empty-handed.

'What have you done?' she asked him in trepidation.

'Burned my letter. Put it on the kitchen fire.'

'Oh, Léon, no, how could you? It meant so much to me, to hold that letter and read it while the battle was raging,' Stefanie said wretchedly.

'Then, here, take this instead,' he pressed the gold medallion into her hand.

'It is your mother's—you wanted her to have it,' she protested.

'Now I want you to have it. Keep it, and think of me sometimes,' he turned away so that she could not see his face.

'You are leaving so soon?' she asked dully. It felt as though a steel band tightened around her heart.

'As the Emperor decides.'

'Then follow your Emperor!' she cried, hardly knowing what she said in her grief and anger. 'Follow Napoleon! Be his loyal Dragoon! Should it matter to me?'

'Does it?' he demanded, looking straight into her eyes.

'Yes—yes—you know it does! What should I do if you ride away and leave me?'

'Then *you* must decide . . .' he said.

The door opened, and the Baroness came in. 'Monsieur de Vaudry,' she took his hand. 'We are once more so much in your debt, and owe you our deepest apologies.'

'It is of no consequence, madame,' he said quietly, as he kissed her hand. 'I am honoured to have been of service to you and to your family.'

The Baroness sat down heavily on the nearest chair and her mask of calm cracked. 'Oh, those children! That poor boy! What shall I do? Magda is so devoted to that unfortunate youth, and if he lives—'

'Mama!' Stefanie begged. 'You cannot part them *now*!'

'No, no. If he lives, they will be married. They talk of it already. They make such plans. It seems there is a Dr Wolfssohn in Vienna. He makes artificial arms and legs—not all of one piece, you understand, but jointed in some way and capable of movement. They hope he will make such an artificial arm for Andreas. They speak of it so confidently. It breaks my heart.'

'They are young, madame, and have each other,' Léon told her earnestly. 'They should be confident.'

'And Ignaz . . .' the Baroness continued wretchedly.

'She means Hofrat von Letzberg,' Stefanie whispered. 'He is Andreas' uncle.'

'How can I write to Ignaz and tell him of this? It will break his heart, too! He was so proud of Andreas.'

'Tell von Letzberg,' Léon said, 'that he may be very proud of his nephew, who is a most gallant soldier, and brave man.'

CHAPTER
THIRTEEN

HAVING established that Andreas was as comfortable as could be expected in the circumstances, Léon took his own departure, promising to see they would not be disturbed, either by soldiers seeking booty, or officers seeking billets. He might have intended this last to include a reference to himself, for that night he did not return.

It began to rain. Stefanie sat up until quite late, listening to the monotonous pitter-patter of the rain-drops on the shutters, and waiting for him, although she knew in her heart that he would not come. She had accomplished what the might of Austria and Russia combined had not been able to do—she had driven him away, perhaps for ever.

At length, further waiting obviously useless, she blew out the candles and went slowly upstairs. Andreas, watched over by the Baroness, still occupied her room. Where Léon slept she had no idea. In some half-ruined cottage, perhaps, doors, window frames and shutters stripped for firewood, so that the rain poured in and the earthen floor turned to mud. Or perhaps beneath the stars themselves, rolled in a sodden blanket by a fire which hissed and spluttered beneath the onslaught of the rain, until it died down, wet, blackened and cold.

She pushed open the door of the room in which he had slept. The moonlight streamed in through the unshut-tered windows and fell across the empty bed. Stefanie sat on the coverlet and smoothed it with her hand, reseeing in her mind his head buriéd in the pillows. At

177

last, with a resigned sigh, she slipped off her shoes, crept under the quilt and fell asleep where Léon had lain the night before.

The next morning she was awoken by a clatter of hoofs and ran downstairs in time to see a party of some twenty Chasseurs *à cheval* of the Guard ride past, in a vivid kaleidoscope of red, green and gold. Their gold-tasselled Hungarian style boots glistened, their immaculate uniforms glittered with braid and their round fur bonnets gave them more the appearance of Russians than of Frenchmen. As if vying with the riders, the horses were beautifully turned out, satin coats brushed till gleaming and saddle harness a show of shining metal and well-buffed leather. In all, a picture of military perfection.

'Escort party,' muttered Wenzel in surly admiration of this splendid sight. 'Someone important is on the move!'

Later they were able to hear clearly the various distant trumpet calls signalling between the advance posts. Stefanie went to see how Andreas progressed, and found him wan and very weak, also in great pain, but remarkably cheerful, despite his sad plight. To her great relief, the wound left by the amputation showed no sign of becoming infected.

'I admire your courage so much, Andreas,' she told him, 'and I want you to know it.'

'I am alive,' he said simply. 'I had rather not lost an arm . . . but it is better than losing a leg. General Kienmayer has but one arm, after all, and far better men than I lost their lives.'

She told him about the mounted escort party which had passed the house and a shadow crossed his face, and some of his optimism faded.

'They exchange emissaries,' he said disconsolately. 'Napoleon presents us with his terms.'

'Isn't that to be expected?' Magda asked from her

perch on the bed. She took Andreas' remaining hand and placed his open palm against her soft cheek. 'Let Bonaparte takes whatever he wants, only let him gather his Grand Army and *go away*!'

Andreas smiled at her wanly, and Stefanie went quietly out of the room. Downstairs in the kitchen, Hanka stood over a great tub of boiling water, energetically drubbing the bloodstained linen from the operation. Stefanie, for want of anything better to do, and wishing to keep her mind from dwelling on Léon, tied on an apron and helped her to carry the sheets out into the garden. Outside everywhere sparkled from the previous night's rain, as if washed like the sheets of all foulness wrought by man, and all afresh to greet the new day.

'Like as not, they'll freeze as stiff as boards!' puffed Hanka, as they struggled to hang the heavy sheets over a line tied between two trees.

Water ran off the linen and dripped onto Stefanie's hair, down her neck and into her sleeves. She uttered an exclamation of disgust. 'These wretched things will never dry!'

'Just stand clear, my dearie. Bless you, but you're more in my way than you're helping. They'll dry, never fear, provided no one comes along and helps himself first! I'll tell Janko to keep an eye on them. All the time those Frenchman are around here, nothing's safe. I'll be glad to see them all gone, and that's a fact. We don't need them coming back, neither.' She tipped up the wash tub and set off with it back into the house.

Stefanie untied the apron and sat down with it rolled up on her lap on the wooden seat beneath an old apple tree. She leaned back listlessly, her eye taking in the garden gate and the empty road beyond. As a little girl she had played beneath this tree. She had climbed up it, and torn her petticoats and been scolded, for young ladies didn't do such things. Worse, once she had got stuck, up above where she now sat, there, in the fork of the two great branches. Stefanie stared upwards now, remembering, and drops of moisture dripped down again onto her upturned face, this time from the branches above. She put up a hand and wiped them away absently. How frightened she had been then, and humiliated too, knowing that she had only herself to blame. Wenzel—then a strapping lad of nineteen—had been fetched from the stables to climb up, grinning from ear to ear, and bring the little lady safely down. Now, once again, she was locked fast in a situation caused partly in the first place by her own temerity. She had behaved again as no well brought up young lady should, this time in giving her heart to a vagabond gentleman of fortune, who had pledged his sword to Napoleon and rode with the army of the French to defeat her country. Once again her own actions had left her frightened. But who would rescue her now?

She rested her head against the gnarled trunk and closed her eyes. Hoofbeats sounded from the road, as a rider came galloping towards the house. 'It will be some emissary en route with a message to the Austrians,' she thought. 'What will they take from us? What will be the price?'

It was cold out here in the garden, and the moisture continued to drip down from the bare branches above, down onto her face, but still she did not move. Not until she felt someone gently take the apron which she held loosely in her hands, and with it wipe the wetness from her brow and cheeks.

She opened her eyes with a start, and stared upwards, up into Léon's face, looking earnestly down at her.

He dropped the apron onto the seat and asked unexpectedly, 'Is he dead?'in a quiet tone.

She was so confused at seeing him there when she had not heard him approach, nor even expected him, that this question only served to bewilder her further, and she replied a little foolishly, 'Who?'

'Young von Letzberg,' he said impatiently. 'Is that why you are sitting out here in the cold wind and weeping? Has he died?'

'No, no!' Stefanie jumped to her feet. 'No, he came through the night very well, the wound is clean and we begin to believe he will recover.' She flushed slightly. 'I wasn't crying. It was all the rain from last night, running down from the branches . . .'

'I see. Not weeping for von Letzberg—nor for me,' he said drily.

'Is that why you have come, Léon? To see if I wept for you?' she flung at him, her uncertainty leading to resentment.

'No!' he retorted savagely. 'I came to bring you news, news for all of you. News of an armistice!'

'An armistice?' she cried, staring at him wildly.

'Yes. Stefanie, don't you see? Can't you understand what it means? Your Emperor Franz has cut himself free from his Russian allies and will make peace with us! Austria and France will be at *peace*!' he repeated urgently.

'I cannot believe it,' she whispered. 'Oh, Léon, I don't dare to believe it! I have never wanted or prayed for anything so much.'

'Then I am perhaps not so unwelcome a visitor,' he said.

'I thought you would never come again,' she managed to utter tremulously through quivering lips.

His saturnine cheeks darkened and then the blood drained from them, leaving them pale beneath their tan. 'You think I could stay away from you?' he burst out suddenly. 'I rode through the Russian pickets to see you for ten minutes in a kitchen, two nights ago. Have you forgotten so soon?' With a lightning movement, he seized her arms and exclaimed, 'And I am here again, because I cannot stay away!

'Stefanie, do you remember that first evening in

Vienna when you played Eve to me? You set yourself to make me want you, and I did want you, I wanted you so much I felt I could not bear to stay in that house with you if you could never be mine. I swore you would be mine, one day. I knew that beneath that snow-white bosom there beat a heart which begged to be awakened, and I vowed I would be the man to awaken it to love. That one belief alone has sustained me in all the days since then, and through everything that has happened. What do you want of me? Anything that is in my power to give you is yours. My name? I would be honoured if you would take it. And I have tried, imperfectly, perhaps, but tried to be patient . . . to wait until the time came when you felt that you could love me. What I cannot do is change myself into a different person. Yet all this time, until yesterday, I hoped . . . I believed you loved me in your heart, and one day I would hear you say it.'

He paused to draw breath, then went on more quietly, 'Yesterday, it seemed as if the world had come to an end for me, and there was nothing but a black void in front of me. The whole French army celebrated, and I alone despaired, because that hope was destroyed, because I thought you would never forgive me for the misfortunes of that young Hussar, as perhaps you never will. I thought that you had never trusted me, and never loved me, because if you had loved me, you would have believed in me enough to come to me when you were in need of help, no matter what the circumstances. I had been so blinded by my own passion for you, you see, that until yesterday I had believed that one day you would see me as other than a death-dealing monster in a foreign uniform. Perhaps I was wrong . . . but I love you still, and need you, Stefanie, and cannot go on alone without you.

'Now I do not know what you think of me, or whether you can ever put out of your mind what I am. All I know is, that I cannot leave here without you. I cannot live without you, and I will not! I cannot deceive you, Stefanie,' he went on quickly, not allowing her to speak. 'I don't say to you, "this peace will last for ever", because of course it will not. But while it lasts there will be time for *us*. Only God knows how much time we have. Perhaps it is all written somewhere in some great book which we cannot read. All *I* know is that, if we part now, we shall never meet again this side of Eternity . . . and what little time I may have, in this world, I would spend with you. Come with me . . . please . . .' he held out his hand towards her.

'But I do love you, Léon!' Stefanie cried out. 'I never meant to make you so unhappy. If only you knew how wretched it has made me! I thought you would never come again, or ever say again you loved me, and, like you, I could see no future for myself without you. If you cannot live without me, then I cannot exist without you. I don't care how long the peace lasts, or if I must struggle through the mud of a dozen battlefields. You do not need to ask me to go with you. I will follow you, whether you want me or not, trudge behind like the soldiers' women if I must, but I shall never leave you again, never, never!'

She flung her arms around him as if she would indeed never let him go, and turned her face up to his, and felt his lips on hers, demanding from her that response she need no longer deny.

The Baroness listened quietly as Stefanie told her, first of the armistice, and then, hesitantly, of her decision.

'You know I would not want to distress you, Mama,' she said, taking her mother's hand. 'Please understand.'

The Baroness stirred slightly, as if she had been lost in her thoughts, and the touch of her daughter's hand had awakened her.

'Understand? From the beginning I've understood.

He meant to win you. I saw it in his face when he first came to our house in Vienna, saw it in his eyes each time he looked at you. And you? Dear child, I knew what was in your heart before you knew it yourself. I knew you would go with him—sooner or later. Some things are decreed by Fate. We must bow to it.' She sighed.

'You were so sure, and yet you did not try to dissuade me?' Stefanie asked her, a little bewildered. 'You only once uttered a word of warning, and that without telling me all this.'

'And what should I have said to you?' the Baroness asked her sharply. 'What could I have told you that you would have understood? You were as innocent of bodily passions as an infant. You, who were always afraid to lose your heart, Stefanie! How could I talk to you of a thing of which you were so ignorant? Should I have told you this was no lovesick boy who could be sent packing, but a man who *would* have what he desired, and would *not* be denied? You would not have understood me. You did not understand him! Experience is the most precious of possessions, but it is gained only at the expense of time, and of pain. That is what I feared most of all, that you would finish with a broken heart.

'Well, if you will go with him, you will go. I will not, cannot, stop you. I know too well that if the heart is given away already, the rest must follow after. Monsieur de Vaudry!' she turned to Léon, who stood silently by, listening.

'Madame?' he asked quietly.

'You will look after my daughter well? I believe she will lead a raggle-taggle kind of life with you. I might as well let her go with a gipsy!'

He smiled slightly. 'I swear it, madame. I will take her to Epernay, to my home. My mother will be overjoyed to welcome a daughter.'

'Stefanie will not stay there, if you do not! If you follow after Napoleon, she will follow after you. God knows where that will lead her. I have but one request to make of you, monsieur.'

'You have but to name it, madame.'

'I would like to see my daughter married by a priest, in my presence.'

'Madame, I swear to you, I always intended—' he began, but she held up a hand to silence him.

'I would make no accusation against your honour, monsieur! But it is my wish, a mother's wish.'

'Oh, Mama,' Stefanie knelt on the floor by her mother's chair and put her arms round her. 'What will you do when I am gone, and Magda is married to Andreas? You will be left alone.'

'Alone? No. I dare say I shall accept the offer of marriage Ignaz von Letzberg has been making me these three years. We have reached the age, he and I, when we should be able to marry to please ourselves. If eyebrows are raised in Vienna, it hardly matters to us! Besides, since he and I must provide some future for Magda and Andreas, we had best do it together. I would have accepted him before now, but, for some reason I have never understood, both you and Magda seemed to have some prejudice against poor Ignaz. I could not ask him to take upon the role of stepfather in such circumstances.'

'But Magda and I never—' Stefanie stammered, overcome with shame. 'We did not think you wished to marry him! We would never have stood between you, if we had known. But we thought—'

'You *thought* that only young people are permitted to fall in love and marry!' the Baroness snorted. 'Young people are all the same, they believe they have a monopoly in such matters! I assure you that in so many ways, the heart is always young!'

The priest's housekeeper received them with evident dismay.

'Father Maximilian is here, indeed, the poor man has just returned and is having a bite to eat. A marriage?' She stared doubtfully at Léon. 'Honourable Baroness, I don't know what to say. I'll fetch him . . .' she backed away, her eyes fixed on the Frenchman as if the presbytery with its well scrubbed tiled floors and waxed furniture was about to be engulfed in sulphurous flames.

'Tell him, we wait for him in the church!' the Baroness called after her. 'I don't know what is the matter with that woman,' she continued briskly to the wedding party, that is to say, to Léon, Stefanie and Magda. 'But let us go into the church.'

They pushed open the church door and went in. Walls and roof were intact, but every piece of glass had been shattered by the reverberations of the cannonade, and the broken fragments lay scattered across the stone floor.

'Take care!' Léon warned, kicking aside some of the debris.

'Really!' exclaimed the Baroness, lifting her skirts with both hands and stepping gingerly across the stone flags. 'Could no one have swept this up? What have they all been doing?'

A small door at the side of the church creaked open and the priest hurried in, clasping his vestments in his arms. He was a little, balding man with spectacles. He peered at them shortsightedly, and exclaimed, flustered, 'Baroness! My housekeeper tells me you want me to marry some young people!'

'I do,' said the Baroness, surveying him critically. His cassock was heavily stained with fresh mud, as though he had been kneeling on the earth.

Conscious of her scrutiny, he began to try and struggle into the rest of his vestments, and rub away the mud at the same time. 'I apologise dear lady, for my appearance, I have just returned . . .'

'So I see,' said the Baroness. 'Did you fall in the mud, Father Maximilian?'

'Oh, no, no, dear lady. I have been on my knees . . .
the dying, you understand . . .' He peered at them in a
pathetic desire for their understanding. 'Austrians, Russians, even among the French not all are without faith,
despite the sad excesses of the Revolution. I have been
to the field hospitals. Many of those unfortunates whose
limbs were amputated yesterday have not survived the
night . . . the conditions, dear lady, cannot be described
to you . . .'

Stefanie put her hands over her face, and the old man
broke off, embarrassed at distressing his visitor.

'We are sorry, Father,' the Baroness said much more
quietly and soberly, 'to disturb you at such a time, and to
bring you from so pressing a task—for a wedding.'

'From grief to joy, so life goes on,' the elderly priest
said, smiling a little up at them. 'We are born, we die, we
are born to life anew. You have the rings?'

'I only have this ring,' Léon murmured, pulling off his
signet ring.

'Wait, Stefanie shall have my ring!' the Baroness
exclaimed, struggling with the gold band which had
encircled her finger for twenty-five years. 'It is a little
tight, perhaps candle wax—ah! I have it.' She managed
to tug the ring free.

'Oh, Mama—the ring Papa gave you—' Stefanie
whispered, her voice choking.

'Your father would wish it so. It has not left my finger
since he placed it there on our wedding day, but leaves it
now for a good purpose.'

'I have spoken to someone on the imperial staff of
you,' Léon said to Stefanie quietly, as, a little later, they
stepped out of the church and into the cold breeze. 'And
he told the Emperor, who, you should understand, likes
to know everything! I am ordered to present you to him.'

'To Napoleon?' she exclaimed.

'Yes. It is a great honour. We must go at once.'

'So soon?' the Baroness wiped away her tears. 'But it

is better so. Farewells are best made quickly. I will go back to the house and pack together your clothes. Come, Magda.'

So this was the man at whose name all of Europe trembled—the 'arch-fiend Bonaparte' of von Letzberg, the 'Corsican upstart' of her mother. Napoleon, Emperor of the French, here surrounded by his aides and those magnificent men of war, his marshals, whose own names conjured up fear and admiration from the Volga to the Tagus. Messengers scurried in and out, all eagerness to accomplish the will of this man, who was the sun around which they all revolved. A man of medium height and stocky build in his mid-thirties, his hair thinning a little and hardly dressed as one would expect of an emperor. All around him were men uniformed like peacocks, but he wore the dark green of the mounted Chasseurs of the Guard, with a plain grey greatcoat cast over his shoulders against the cold.

He had leant his elbows on a table of inlaid walnut, brought here and pressed into service as a desk, and, with his chin resting on his hands, his gaze flickered rapidly over the mass of papers scattered across it. Amongst them lay his hat, plain, even a little battered, with neither gold nor silver lace.

An aide whispered in his ear, and the Emperor lifted his head and looked straight at Léon and Stefanie. Now none could have been in any doubt in whose presence they stood. The eyes alone told it, dark, lustrous, lively, keen, shrewd. Before that piercing scrutiny, with its undertones of sensuality and cruelty, Stefanie quailed, and curtsied respectfully.

'I am much pleased by this marriage,' the Emperor told her kindly, smiling, and apparently wishing to put her at her ease. 'I see it as a symbol, the true friendship of our nations. I have never wished to make war on Austria. I declared this to your soldiers after Ulm. I have assured His Majesty, the Emperor Franz, of it. No one is more glad than I of the forthcoming peace.'

'Yes, sire,' Stefanie said. 'Thank you.'

He leaned forward slightly. 'You will tell your family, your friends, in Vienna, that I have said so.'

'Yes, sire.'

So, you will make me your messenger? she was thinking. She felt the pull of the spell this fascinating man cast, but she knew she could never be as wholeheartedly devoted to him as those about him, or see him as Léon did. There seemed to be something calculating about the man, for all his friendly tone and smile. It is like that grey coat, and battered hat, she thought. It is done deliberately, they say 'I am Emperor. I do not need fine clothes. Those are for lesser mortals, such as all of you.'

The Emperor turned his attention to Léon now. 'Well, Major de Vaudry,' he said cheerfully, and a stir ran around the surrounding entourage like a ripple from a pebble cast into water. 'This has been a great victory for us. It is my finest. I have told the army: 'My children! Soldiers of the *Grande Armée*! Henceforth it will suffice for each one of you to say, *I was at Austerlitz*! and anyone who hears him will reply, *there goes a hero*!'

He paused, and for a moment the fine, lustrous eyes seemed fixed upon some inner vision, and Stefanie's impressions of him were thrown into confusion once more, and she did not know what to think of this strange man, so enigmatic, intriguing, inspiring and yet dangerous.

Unexpectedly, Napoleon said, 'If you have a son, you will name him for me. You have my permission!'

As they left the room, she heard him observe to a harassed looking man in a fine uniform, 'Madame de Vaudry is a handsome woman.'

When they had regained the open air, and no one could overhear them, Stefanie exclaimed, 'He made a mistake! He called you "Major".'

'The Emperor does not make mistakes. It means I am promoted.' He gave a short laugh. 'Though I shall never know whether it is on account of my valour, or my marriage!'

'Would you mind very much if it were on account of me? I can hardly believe it.'

'The Emperor approves of you,' he smiled at her. 'I shall have to watch out. You have taken his eye. Did you not hear him express his admiration to Caulaincourt?'

'I did. But I am a married woman and impervious to compliments, even from emperors. Would he really promote you for that reason?'

'He means to do us a kindness,' Léon said earnestly. 'My promotion, it is a wedding present. It is his generosity.'

'I require neither his compliments nor his wedding gifts. I want only you.'

He lifted her up onto the waiting horse. 'Me you have always, come what may . . .'

He took the reins from his groom and mounted his own horse. As they rode away, the trumpets of the Grand Army, signalling the arrival of Austrian emissaries, pealed out from near at hand, and the horses threw up their heads and pricked their ears.

'A wedding march!' Léon said enthusiastically, leaning across and taking her hand. 'We shall have no other, yet no one could wish more illustrious music. They are the voice of Fate which throws open the gates to our future. We have but to pass through—come!'

Side by side, they rode across the deserted battlefield, the voices of the victorious trumpets growing ever more distant.